RESCUING THE UNSEELIE KING

Faetales Novella #3

Poppy Minnix

One Night Reads

DEDICATION

To stubborn girlies.
Stand your ground.
The world needs your strength.

CONTENTS

INTRODUCTION

Hello lovers of fantasy and spice!

Welcome to book 3 in the Faetales series! Just like the others in the series, this spicy fae romantasy is a short story (2-hour average for reading) and has darker themes with high spice levels. It also links heavily to the previous two novellas. Reading them in order will help with the quick pacing and overall storyline, though each can standalone. If you'd rather just jump in or need a refresher, here's a quick breakdown to get things rolling...

- The Seelie are iridescent-winged faeries, small and delicate in stature. Most have magic abilities and, like some fae species, many can create impressive glamours (see definition below). Seelie like to think of themselves as the good fae because they're kind to humans and other creatures, and they avoid conflict. But they have some dreadful traditions like The Springfest Sprint—a mate-claiming race for those who have come of age and haven't yet bonded with another, and arranged marriages with magical bonding instead of natural mate-bonding. They are possessive of what's theirs, including friends and mates.

- The Unseelie are another type of faery, though they're a little bigger, have bat-like wings, and a dark side that arises when they have intense emotions like fear, rage, or lust. That makes their eyes go crimson, their fangs drop, and shadows darken certain areas of their bodies, making their features appear sharper and more dangerous. Most of them also have a variety of magic abilities, and they're great at creating and taking down territory wards. They have rules of tradition when courting a mate, but it's not unusual for them to be polyamorous.

- Both types of fae have courts—kingdoms with kings and queens, princes, princesses, dukes, etc. They all have their own processes of ruling over their kind and keeping their territories organized.

  - Seelie courts: Spring, Summer, Autumn, Winter.

  - Unseelie courts: Crown, Northern, Enforcer, West Wind, Hillock.

- There have been and will be lots of different fae-folk mentioned along the way—satyrs, Boggarts, Brownie kin, trolls, leshy, dryads, nymphs, and more. There is so much amazing lore about these fae beings and I'm inspired by some of that, but also create my own lore versions which will continue to build through the series.

- Time! The faeries don't use the human standard of time like minutes, months, and years. They use "flaps/flutters" for something like a second, "moon/moon cycle" for a month, and "full rotation/rotation" for a year. They use decade (10 rotations), century (100 rotations) and millennium (1000 rotations).

- Glamours are a vision some fae can cast to confuse or impress. They can disguise themselves as characters did in The Springfest Sprint and Faetales shorty, Go Ahead and Steal My Heart, create imaginary animals like snakes and rabbits, or even make a full scene that an enemy could get lost in like a fake forest or cave. Some fae are better at glamours than others—Ember is a glamour-champion in The Springfest Sprint.

CATCH UP INFO — SPOILER ALERT FOR BOOK 1 & 2...
- Book one, The Springfest Sprint, starred Princess Ember of the Seelie Spring Court and Prince Typhon of the Unseelie Crown Court. They met when Ember was running from the males of her court during her people's traditional mate claiming race, the Springfest Sprint, and hid in the cave he was hanging out in. They had a fling, and Prince Typhon entered the race to compete for her while courting her according to Unseelie tradition so the bonding would be valid. He won her, and she accepted his courting. They moved into the Crown Court castle to help run it since King Kage, Typhon's brother, has been detained by the Rioch nymphs.

- Book two, Stealing the Bogeyman's Bride, brought in Auralia and Donovan from the Unseelie Crown Court, and explored the lore of the Bogeyman—the only known fae that can lie. Auralia believed she was bonded to the Bogeyman who returned for her after a decade of minimal check-ins. She went into heat after the Bogeyman destroyed a trinket she'd used to prevent that from happening, but it was Donovan who set it off. He stole her from the Bogeyman, and while in her heat phase, he got her to confess that the Bogeyman killed the Crown Court King (Typhon and Kage's father) with her help, but Donovan and Auralia formally bonded as well. Auralia went back to fight the Bogeyman when he attacked her friends and Donovan in a dream state, and when they came to, the Unseelie Crown court followed her into a gruesome battle. They won, but Auralia was injured and in trouble because of her involvement with past treasons. At the end of the book, Auralia is being held in the barracks (though Donovan won't leave her side and made her prison more like a luxury hotel room), while they await the return of King Kage, so he can decide her fate.

They are all involved in this book, as well as the Grimm brothers—the gentry and his second from the Enforcer Court, and Jinimadora—another Bogeyman spy who was also living in the Unseelie Crown castle as a liaison. They all helped win the battle against the Bogeyman and his minions.

Now for those trigger warnings (Look away if you prefer to be surprised!)...

...

...

Last chance...

If you're not up for reading about a graphic sexual descriptions and violence, off-page MMC sexual assault, and fate that refuses to be fair about getting certain fae together, whether or not they're interested, this is your warning!

Happy reading!

Poppy

CHAPTER ONE

WIDOW WITH A PLAN

WILLOW

Those Unseelie-eating beasts better be here. I wouldn't have agreed to rescue King Kage if I didn't think they were.

But I'm starting to doubt with all this silence. Rioch is nice enough for a forest territory, though I prefer areas with more open fields lined with an array of flowers instead of the same four types of trees on repeat. Plus, it's easier to see danger in open spaces.

The dryads ignore me from their homes within pines and firs, and, so far, no hellhounds have presented themselves. It's a rumor that the nymphs are using the creatures as guards since they detained the king of the Unseelie Crown Court, but all my hope rides on their presence. Murdering an Unseelie is not something I'm likely to be capable of doing. I only wish for it to be done.

The hole in my heart still gapes for my mate. Flint had been out of the territory at the time and most Seelie are homebodies, only wishing to occupy their areas in peace. If a life is taken outside the defended region... well, they shouldn't have left. Those who believe that didn't lose a mate though, did they?

I still cannot believe Princess Ember bonded with one of them during our traditional event, the Springfest Sprint. That was a crinkle to the wing—not that she understood how much it pained me. So few do.

And now the royals set up a portal for easier travel between the territories. As if there wasn't spilt blood between us. As if I've forgotten what their king did.

But there was a shining bright gem among the muck of that moment, because when the Unseelie announced his name—Prince Typhon Redrek Jenderos—I knew fate had given me an opportunity to ease the pain that has strangled me for so many cycles.

Jenderos.

A prince of the Crown Court provided a link to my worst enemy, his brother, as if determined by fate. I could have laughed if it wouldn't have alerted the crowd that something was terribly off about me. My epiphany unveiled a plan, though I've kept quiet out of necessity.

My people would have stopped me.

The Unseelie would have killed me as they did my mate, instead of welcoming me into their Keep for the past moon—letting the harmless Seelie widow learn their strengths and weaknesses. They trust me. Foolish for fae, but I did good work. And now I will finally gain justice for my slain mate.

Rubbing at my chest doesn't make the tension go away.

And then the most blessed sound fills the forest. A screechy growl. Another farther off.

I grin and perch on a tree.

The creatures wander like beige, furless panthers among the underbrush. No wonder I've had no run-ins with birds, snakes, or even come across a beetle or dragonfly. All creatures have holed themselves away protectively in their hiding spots because death looms on the forest floor.

Perfect.

Now, I only need to get the king out of the nymph coven, remove whatever protection they've given him, and the beasts will take care of my retribution.

"What pretty monsters you are," I whisper when one turns a wild, orange eye on me.

It snorts and continues on.

The Unseelie were right. I'm safe here. Assumed good and gentle. Here to help my grieving process. I've grieved. And all that's left to heal my heart is revenge. Then maybe I'll see a different future from the one I lost.

It was supposed to be easy after Flint and I bonded. My family finally looked at me with something that could be considered pride. I'd found my life's path—had my existence laid out among fields of flowers, mead socials, and children I would have loved far more than I was.

That is all gone because of a king with too much power. It's still so surreal.

Dropping from the tree branch, I flit toward where the main coven building should be, according to the map I memorized. Sure enough, the thatched roof stands out inside a grouping of small huts, stone buildings, and holly bushes.

My target lies within. If I'm very lucky, maybe the king will already be dead.

CHAPTER TWO

SUCH A PITY

WILLOW

I tug at the sleeve of my boxy mourning garb as we pass by doors marked with unfamiliar symbols, and hope Kissip, the pretty nymph leading me down a circular stick-woven corridor, can't scent my nervousness. Not that it matters much. Being a widow in a nymph brothel is a logical excuse for anxiety.

She's my height—which is tall for a Seelie. From my understanding, nymph magic allows them to be any size to fit the fae they're around. Better to seduce them, I'm sure.

"I expected to need to fly everywhere," I say as we turn a corner. "Do all the Rioch nymphs remain in small fae form?"

"Someone is making nervous talk." Kissip gives my shoulder a playful nudge. "It's easier to hide our towns and fit within a territory without drawing undue attention when you don't take up as much room. Kind of like you all do." She bites her lip and looks at me from under her lashes. "I'll make plans to visit your territory soon."

I've been told a nymph's appeal is a lure to all. I'm not lured. Then again, I'm broken because of the lingering mate bond. Why the gods cursed me with a reminder of my past mate and the future I'll no longer have is beyond me.

She signals to my dress. "I understand why you came here. There's nothing like pleasure in the hands of nymphs and the company we keep. We understand and accept more than most fae. How long has it been?"

"Three cycles."

She stumbles to a stop. "Since you've been pleasured?"

My face heats. "By another? Yes." Not that self-pleasure has been all that pleasurable. More like taking care of a need when I didn't want a partner that brought up my loss like they were there to do me a favor. All the Spring fae seem more intent on pitying a widow than seeing me as a desirable faery.

Her brown eyes go wide. "And your bonded mate was a male?" She steps in front of me, looking me up and down. "Maybe you'd be interested in trying someone else?"

When I glance over her face, down to her pale-yellow diaphanous shirt and pants with fresh eyes, she takes one of my red spiral curls and wraps it around her finger.

I shake my head, tugging my hair from her grasp. "I've been with females." It's not a lie, but that was before Flint. "Those experiences have been enjoyable, but today, I'd like to see a male." A specific male.

The difficulty in running a plan like this is not lying. I'd give myself away if I told them I wanted to have sex with a captured king, then fell to the ground in agony from the liar's curse. As of now, all I'm doing is giving the general situation and Kissip is filling in her own ideas of the story.

"Another day, then." She lifts her pointed chin. "Right this way."

She lifts a latch and a twig-thatched door with an orange symbol creaks open, showing a small bedroom.

A male dryad reads a book in a pile of silks. His blazing yellow eyes pop up to me, and he looks annoyed to be disturbed. "What is it, Kissip?" His voice is as rough as bark.

"Interested in entertaining a Springy?" my guide asks.

"No." His eyes drop back to his book.

It is good that he doesn't want me, but I pretend to be struck, sinking my shoulders down and letting my wings droop.

Kissip closes the door and wrinkles her nose. "He's grumpy. I thought his quietness might be a good match, but perhaps you need more fun in your life. Shall we?"

She continues down the hallway, and I follow, taking in the layout and trying to peek into any gap between twigs, hoping for a glimpse of the Unseelie king. When she pauses at another door, I clasp my fingers in front of me.

The two satyrs she reveals are as handsome as Seelies, but they have the legs of a goat. I don't mind the fur. It's probably quite warm at night. One stands and clops over on hooves. "A widow?" His pitying look stings my chest.

I shake my head. "I cannot be with anyone that will pity me for what has happened. It makes me think too much—takes me from the moment." That is nothing but the truth and the reason I haven't been with another since Flint's death. I'm not a pet to be coddled and fixed. I want someone who will need me as is, though that's not what I'm here for today.

The satyr's brows furrow, but he displays open arms, bows his head, and steps backward.

Kissip leans against the wall, looking me over. "What are you looking for?"

I'd smile if it wouldn't give me away. "Someone big, who isn't afraid of hurting me, and who doesn't care that I'm a widow." My description is spot on. Unseelie are huge, and the king couldn't care less about who he hurts, nor will he care that he's the one who made me a widow.

I only hope they'll allow it.

Will the nymph at least give me the status of the king? If she says there's no one like that here, then the royal Unseelie is dead and buried elsewhere or has left. Kissip raises a blond eyebrow. "And what are you willing to give for that?"

And there's the nymph's trap. I'm a little surprised she's even bringing up a payment, considering she'll probably attempt to trap me or my power either way. "Anything." Not a lie.

It's not smart to give an open favor. Whole families have become indebted to other fae because they tossed around promises. But I'm done for after this, anyway. As soon as the king is dead, the Unseelie army will kill the nymphs, invalidating any favor I grant them, or the nymphs will kill me for ruining their plans for Kage, or the Crown Court will catch and dispose of me, as the Unseelie are so apt at doing. If I get through this and return home, maybe Flint's and my families will see me as a hero, and I can move forward.

Kissip tips her head toward the hallway. "Follow me."

Chapter Three

THE KING

WILLOW

She takes me down another short corridor with a rune-marked solid door at the end. She twists the handle, and we step into the small room made of woven twigs.

The loveliest Unseelie I've ever seen lies back on a pile of silks on the floor. He looks made of stone with sharply sculpted features. His smirking lips are so defined, they make me have visions of dragging my fingertips along the ridges of the deep pink flesh.

The scent in the room must be him. It's warmly spiced with pine, but also sweet. My mouth waters. I trail my tongue over my teeth, then the roof of my mouth, and swallow hard. What in the nine realms is my problem?

He has one arm tucked behind his head of light blond hair that's tousled and wavy over his shoulders and chest, and the other is below a silk sheet, moving rhythmically up a huge—oh, merciless devil.

My wings give an embarrassing buzz of excitement. I suck in a breath, pivoting away from the tempting sight.

"He's beautiful, isn't he?" Kissip says, still staring toward the Unseelie. "Pure blood. Royal. Exceptional in the art of pleasure."

I want to scratch her eyes out. Wrap her up in the magical fist I can conjure and squeeze until her bones snap. She shouldn't have touched what wasn't hers. Not that it matters. It doesn't. Of course, she's touched him. Every nymph in the territory probably has, and that's fine. I hope he enjoyed his final days.

Kissip leans close and my skin crawls, but, like a good widow who's only here to relearn the art of sensuality, I hold still. "He's the queen's personal bedmate, but she needs to share him more." Her grin is wicked, and now I have another problem to deal with, because I'm fairly certain I'm being used to instigate a nymph fight. She flicks her eyebrows. "She shouldn't be too angry with a Seelie favor in her grasp. If that is still on the table?"

That doesn't mean the queen won't be furious. I need to hurry this up. Get him and me out to the openness of the forest.

I glance back at the breath-stealing enemy. "What's his name?"

The brightest green eyes meet mine and hold firm. For a moment, I don't want this alluring monster to be the king. I don't like that his stare makes warmth bloom in my chest and other areas.

Lust is the worst of emotions.

"Kage." His eyes go half lidded and he drops his head back against the wall.

"Kage," I whisper back. The Unseelie king I am to rescue. The one I aim to kill.

The movement under the sheets picks up, and his groan tightens every muscle between my legs. It's not right, but bodies are unintelligent. It's only a biological reaction and means nothing.

Here goes. "Yes. I offer a favor." Magic slides over me, sealing the deal. I don't have a clue what they'll ask of me, but if I'm very lucky, there won't be time.

"Accepted." Kissip opens the door and backs out. "I shall inform the queen of the pact. Enjoy your time under the protection and pleasure of the nymphs of Rioch."

She closes the door, and I blow out a long breath. Phase one complete. And now I explain—

Strong hands grip my sides and turn me.

I open my mouth to scream, but lips crash down onto mine, muffling my voice. While something like elation explodes within my chest, sending tendrils of magic flowing through my veins—he's too close. The danger. He'll kill me as he did my mate. *Fangs.* Violent, vicious—

I shove my magic outward.

Kage hits the wall on the other side of the room, sending a spray of cracked twigs scattering, then lands in a naked heap on a red and blue rug.

Sucking in tiny breaths, I try to expand my lungs while wondering if I already killed the king.

He twitches and slowly lifts his head. His light brows furrow, and then his eyes widen and turn the red of Unseelie rage as he looks around the room. "Where am I?"

CHAPTER FOUR

THE UNEXPECTED INCONVENIENT PERFECT THING

KAGE

The Seelie across the room presses back into the wall as she gasps for breath. Her hair is a wild mess of crimson curls that are bigger than she is. The shape of her eyes is nothing short of artful sadness; her nose, adorably tilted up in a queenly fashion. Her eyes blaze purple, and it tethers me to sanity in this unfamiliar place.

Mates will do that.

We're in a twig-built box that smells like the Seelie across from me—daffodil and spring heather, river rock and clouds. There are other scents, but my mind tells me they don't matter at all. She matters. I matter. What happens between us matters.

But I'm naked. And so hard.

"By the gods." I scramble for a silken sheet lying on the floor. There's a tiny bathing chamber in an alcove, but when I rush toward it to see my garments are within the small cabinet, she jolts, thumping her head against the wall.

I quickly wrap the sheet around my waist and approach my Seelie, but she scrambles sideways.

"Shh." I take a knee on the floor in front of her. "Where are we, my flower? Explain what happened."

She bares her teeth at me and scrambles farther away.

I crawl along the dusty floor, following her. "You must explain. I need to know why I'm here, what happened, and... how I don't remember my mate."

Her eyes widen. "No." She appears so scared. Why would she be scared when I can protect her from anything?

"No?" I ask.

She shakes her head vigorously. "No. You can't be. I'm... it's not possible. It's—" Her jaw tightens, and she shakes her head even more, closing her eyes. Her pain and panic hits me viscerally, making my fangs drop and my claws extend.

"You don't remember either, then?" The protective Unseelie part of me fully engages, making my voice a demon's grumble. I reach for her, running my knuckles along the soft, tawny skin of her calf. Sparks of pleasure make gooseflesh rise along my arm.

She gasps, flicks her fingers and some unseen entity grips my torso and flings me from her.

I extend my wings, but instead of halting, air whooshes through the thin membranes, and I hit the wall, leaving a dent of cracked twigs before I land on my feet. I pull the slipping sheet up my hips, un-tuck, then re-tie it.

My mate stands but continues to push herself against the wall. She's quite tall and as beautiful as a field of poppies at sunset.

"Are you injured?" I ask, taking a step forward.

"No. You are."

I glance to where she's looking and find my wings. My stomach lurches as I stretch them out. Someone carved shapes and letters into the membrane, allowing air to pass through, making them not only useless, but a mockery. There are variations of hearts, symbols, and slices in different stages of healing, some nearly closed and others so fresh, they're crusted and scabbed. On my right wing are the words, "Property of Ornia." The carved words are hard to read as it's healing, but it's there, on my goddamned wing.

My face heats, and I tuck my wings so my mate doesn't have to look at the untruth. "The nymph queen will pay dearly."

My mate swallows hard, but nods.

"Is that where we are?" I tug at my hair and crinkle my brow. Did my hair grow? Everything is so fuzzy. Memories and logic come forth just to flit away and become ungraspable.

"You do not know?" Confusion lies over her beauty, and I wish to kiss it away.

I step closer.

A knock comes from my right, but there are only walls in that direction.

My mate springs into action, gliding across the room on sparkling round wings that glimmer the color of her eyes. She lands daintily on the makeshift bed on the floor and begins jumping, disrupting the silks, and creaking the twig floor. She moans and my cock wakes back up.

The knock sounds again. "Willow?" asks a feminine voice. "There was a crash. Did it come from in there?"

"Willow," I purr. How could I not remember my mate's name?

"Busy," Willow says, in this breathy way I want to hold on to, hear again, over and over. "Don't—" She gasps and moans. "Don't come in. Everything is fine."

She's too distracting. How would someone come into this room? Why wouldn't we want them to? I need to figure it out, but what's under the odd gray sack she's wearing is far more intriguing. Exploring every inch of her with my tongue is pressing.

"Are you sure?" the voice says, muffled behind me. "Kage?"

My mate rolls her hand through the air in a "get on with it" motion, so I stride the few steps to her. But when I reach for her, she stops jumping and flattens back against the wall again.

"Are you afraid of me?" I ask.

"Kage?" The voice is harder now.

"Pretend you're... *with* me." She crinkles her nose as if that's not the most appealing thing to ever want.

I place a hand on the wall next to her. "I don't want to pretend."

"Kage," she whispers in a growling voice, but she eyes my lips, and heat floods through my center and my wings. She needs me.

There's an intrusive gasp behind me, and when I glance in that direction, an unfamiliar nymph stands in the enclosed room. She inhales, but the moment her shriek begins, my mate growls and the nymph flies sideways into the wall, dropping to the floor in a heap. She groans and goes silent.

Willow slips under my arm, rushing away from me to approach the nymph, and pulls off the fae's rings and an amulet from around her neck. "We might need these."

This is all so confusing. "For what?"

"We're leaving." She strides towards the wall, then disappears.

"Willow?" I leap to follow, stopping when I come to a wall.

"Come on." Her voice calls to me as if she's standing close, but she's not there.

I push at the wall, but it's only hard, woven sticks.

"What are you doing? We have to get out of here."

"I can't."

CHAPTER FIVE

DECEPTION AMONG ALLIES

KAGE

Following the wall, I push at the tightly woven twigs, panic ripe within me to be near my mate again. I press a spot on the wall that isn't as hard. It's spongy, but impenetrable. Enchanted. I shake my head and step back.

Willow reappears in front of me.

I reach for her, but she quickly slips to the side and backs away. I ball my hands, my claws digging into my palms. "What is going on?"

She points to the spot with a little give. "You can't pass through the door?"

"What door?"

"And there's the enchanted ward." Her wings and shoulders sink. "They're quite determined to keep you here, aren't they?"

"Why?" I don't have a clue why someone would use a mystical barrier to keep another in. It's usually the other way around. Keeping fae out of your business is a necessity.

She pulls the handful of jewelry from a pocket in her shift, holds it out, then flinches when our skin grazes.

I grip the rings as she pulls away. "You are afraid of me." My chest tightens at the thought. The mate bond is the highest of fae wishes. It strengthens us, lightens our spirit, and warms us with contentedness. Though she is new to me, I already grasp that those rumors are true. This is a moment to explore, not run.

"We just need to get out of here." She hardens her jaw.

"I agree." I shove the rings on my fingers as far as they will go, which is my first knuckle.

"Now try to walk through," she says.

There's no give to the wall. I rub my temples. Everything is dizzying and my mate's scent is intoxicating in this small room. "There's nothing there, and I can't concentrate."

"What do you last remember?" she asks.

"All I can think of right now is you."

She glares.

I study each ring on my fingers. "Not the romantic kind, I see."

"Not now, Kage."

"Later, then?" I ask, raising an eyebrow.

Her consistent glare makes me want to work to discover what other expressions she makes. "Focus. You're in the nymph coven. They have been keeping you hostage and you're needed back at your court."

I blink and shake my head. "That can't be right. I..." What did I do last? "There was a letter asking for a discussion about an alliance from the nymph queen."

She points to my wing. "Queen Ornia?"

I open my wing and lose the air in my lungs. I've been marred with symbols and the most disturbing words. "Does this say 'Property of Orn—'" I clench my jaw tight. No wonder my mate is upset. "It's not true, Willow. I know nothing about this." I give my wings a flap and rage swirls through me as the air whooshes through an array of carvings. Are those... hearts? What in the nine realms happened to me?

Willow rubs her forehead. "You already forgot. We have to get out of here." Just as I tuck my wings, she rushes forward and puts her hand on the gray membrane. "Wait." She smooths out the skin as I open it.

Tingles of warmth travel all over me. "That feels... exceptional."

"It's a rune."

I jerk when she pokes at a sore spot. "Ow."

She curls her fingers against her palm. "They carved a rune into your flesh that matches the one on the door. That's the ward holding you here. I don't... I'm not sure how to fix that without hurting you."

Mates don't hurt each other. Not on purpose.

"Not having it there will let me follow you?"

"That would be my guess."

Stepping back from my mate, I inhale, fold my wing toward me, hold my breath, and slash the membrane with my claws. With a roar, I drop to my knees. The pain in my wing is like I dipped it in a fire that's now rushing up my back.

How would anyone have been able to carve these markings into me without... I squeeze my eyes shut and try to hold tight to my monster as I remember more after reading the queen's letter in the comfort of my Keep's office. I remember leaving by myself for a quick weekend at a trusted nymph coven.

There was a dinner. I caught up with a couple of familiar nymphs. We spent the night together, but were interrupted by the arrival of the new queen. And then…

My claws scar the floor, streaking dark blood along the wood. "It was a kiss."

Willow has both hands over her mouth as she stares at me with wide eyes. She lowers them and clears her throat. "A kiss?"

"Ornia," I say through grit teeth. "Welcomed me to her coven with a kiss. That's the last thing I remember." So, there's truth to a nymph's enchantment, though it was stupid of her to use it on me. That deception will be dealt with.

Willow's purple eyes flash to a deep blue as she looks toward an unconscious nymph on the floor. She steps toward the doorway.

I startle. There is a door.

She tilts her head. "You see it now?"

I nod.

"We have to be as quiet as possible." She opens the door. "Follow me."

The nymph coven tricked me as they posed as allies, harming me, and scaring my mate—who I wish I remembered meeting.

That doesn't warrant going quietly.

CHAPTER SIX

FOR WHOM THE SHAME BELL TOLLS

WILLOW

Pleasure dances over my skin every time Kage steps close to me, and then shame shoves it away with righteous force. How could he—a murderer—be my mate, especially when I still hold power from being bonded to Flint? What kind of cruel game is fate playing?

I can stop it, though. The plan can stay the same.

Sure, it might make my stomach curdle and my blood go icy to envision Kage meeting the hellhounds of the forest, but I only feel that way because of this horrendous mystical prank. It will only last until he's gone. Then everything will return to how it was, except I'll be free from this incessant rage.

I dash along the path Kissip led me until I get to the door to the outside. Then, I turn to Kage and whisper as low as I can. "There are four different huts we need to pass to get to the woods and a supply bag I hid."

His blazing red eyes hold mine, though they're slightly vacant.

He has been through much.

I shake away that thought because so have I. Because of him. "We could hide in the last two temporarily if we needed to, but let's try to get past the holly bushes and into the woods without raising attention. If we can do that, we should be good until they discover you're missing."

Then we can head toward the area where I saw the hellhounds and slow down. However, if the nymphs catch us first... I'll have a choice to make—use the amulet to call back to the Unseelie, signaling that Typhon can pull the king back to the safety of the Crown Court, or warring with the nymphs, possibly losing my life, and having Kage returned to the coven. Let's hope that decision doesn't need to be made.

"Then, let's go." There's something in his eyes that sends a chill of alert up my spine. His gaze may be vacant, but he's vibrating with energy. The past months' memories may be coming back to him, fueling an inner rage. He's a king that seems to be respected for his rationality and good temper, so I'm sure he's excellent at hiding his true self. He dips his head, getting too close. "What is it, mate?"

Or it's the tightness of a bond that wants more.

I'm reeling too, but there's no time for tiptoeing around truths. "You're... attention grabbing."

He's taut with muscle, and his hair and face are so eye-catching, I can't stop staring, even as he moves closer. When his lips come so close to mine, the heat and sweet scent of him makes me want to swoon into his body.

I lunge backward. "No time." No anything. Never. Not with him.

He growls behind me, but it doesn't instill fear like it should.

Lust puddles between my legs. I growl too. This is beyond unfair. I can't comprehend how this happened, but I won't get the chance to process or fulfill my destiny unless we escape. I twist the handle, but the door doesn't open. It doesn't open the next time I try, or when I shove at it, or smash a shoulder into it.

Kage's warm hand on my hip makes me halt all movement, and his rich scent encompasses me so thoroughly that I forget to move away from his touch. He reaches by me and taps the handle with his ringed knuckles. The door creaks open, spilling late day sun into the corridor. "Good thinking, mate." He wiggles his fingers.

I'm clearly not thinking at all anymore.

His chest presses against my shoulder as he leans to look outside. "Clear." When I only stand there, immersed in scent and pleasure tingles, he slides around me.

I jerk back.

Kage sighs and steps outside. "Come, mate."

Teeth and fists clenched, I follow. Movement to my right has me pushing at Kage, who speeds up. The nymphs in the distance laugh and chatter, and when we make our way between the two huts and slip behind a clump of grass, I release my held breath.

The left hut's door swings open and I duck, finding myself pressed against Kage's side. I want to run. My muscles shake to do so.

But then, a close-by nymph laughs. "How do you think the widow is doing with the King?"

I close my eyes. Well, that's out now.

"Kissip said the poor thing looked like she might be ill. And no one wanted her. Good thing it doesn't matter if the king wants her or not.

He'll do her, anyway. And we needed a Seelie favor with how badly things are going with the Unseelie."

Peeking open an eye, I find Kage staring hard at me with... that better not be pity. I glare at him and lean away. I should make a break for it. They probably won't see me.

The nymph's laugh is light, and yet malicious. "Ornia will flay Kissip when she finds out."

"Well, Ornia shouldn't be keeping him all to herself. It's not fair. Everyone knows she's not a true queen."

That raises my eyebrows. Maybe we can wait for one more moment since they're talking about important stuff now. As much as I don't care, stoking discord within the nymph coven might help us. The only thing the Unseelie know about Ornia is that she's young for a queen and started reaching out to Kage a little over a cycle ago.

"Not everyone knows that. Or they're waiting to see what she's planning next, since she's the one who got the king here."

Kage stares between slightly swaying grass blades, eyes red and narrowed.

"No one can question her role until the An Nasc Iontach is complete."

The king's gaze flits to me, and whatever he sees there—what I'm sure is truth and resolve—makes his jaw tighten further. Even with the situation surrounding me, I'm still not sure I trust the myth of the divine bonding event. It's likely, though, especially with the recent knowledge I've gained through the Unseelie.

The mythical Bogeyman had locked Auralia, Kage's executive officer—his second—to him with lies because he believed the An Nasc Iontach would make her produce his spawn. He's a powerful being, the only known fae the liar's curse didn't affect, and he already had a boggart mate. But the fact that he believed the mystical event was nearly underway is an argument that normalcy in the realm is about to be uprooted.

The nymph snorts. "But, after? She's going to have to watch her back. Not that I'd do anything."

"No, never." The other nymph laughs.

"But I can tell you, when the moons line up, I'm going to be first in line outside the king's chamber."

"There's going to be a lottery because he'll only be able to service so many and survive."

They all need to be fried. Squished. Drowned. Though that last one's not possible. They're masters of nature, especially water, and would only divert the flow or somehow use it to their advantage.

Kage slowly turns his gaze on me again and studies my eyes.

Heat floods into my chest, making me want to lean toward him. I wince and try to edge away, except that disturbs the grass. I freeze.

"Who knows? Perhaps he'll accidentally kill Ornia with sex before then."

"She seems to be trying hard to do just that, but it's rumored that he's not responding to her. She keeps having to spell him, and even then?"

"That's going to—"

And the voices fade too much to be heard.

I peek up and over the grass, whisper, "We can go," and bolt toward the large stone storage buildings. I keep my wings tightly tucked so their glimmer doesn't pull attention.

Kage moves behind me so silently that when I reach the tree line and slip behind an elm, I expect him to do the same. He doesn't. Because he's no longer behind me.

He throws the rings from his fingers, and crouches next to the larger of the two buildings. One hand is on the building and he's sunk the other into a mud puddle at his feet. What is he—

The building lists sideways, caving in like it's melting, and I'm left watching wide-eyed as he moves to the other. The first continues to topple, or sludge into itself until Kage is knee-deep in mud. The other building starts the same process as soon as Kage's fingertips brush whatever the first building has become. Stones crunch and twigs crack under the pressure of the liquified storage buildings as the huts crumple inward.

Muffled screams have me covering my mouth in shock.

Kage wades toward me, looking like a glorious, yet livid, mud-monster. The moment he gets to the tree line, shouts start in the distance.

"Run." I take off, signaling to him to follow.

He picks up his pace.

I take to the air and check our path. Clear, unlike behind us, with the growing number of nymphs exploring their new lake of mud. "What did you do?"

Kage weaves his way through the underbrush. "Gave them a taste of what's coming for them."

Chapter Seven

The Hunt

KAGE

My mate is a widow.

That pains me in ways I never expected. I am sad for her, yet glad she is mine, and yet also hurt that she wasn't meant to be mine alone, which gives me guilt because she lost her bonded mate.

I already can't imagine not being near her. She must harbor pure agony from her loss.

I've never bonded, and few get a second chance unless by false, magical means. The magic shifting between us is not at all false, though. She's opened a new pleasurable facet of myself I wasn't aware of. Even the strongest of magic couldn't fake this. But I have a sinking sensation in my gut that she may not feel the same way.

I don't even know her. I only know that I want to inhale her neck, taste her body and blood, and make sure she understands I am fully hers. Not... *property of a nymph.*

I will kill the fake queen before her coven sisters have the chance and set new fae rules for them. No one else needs to experience the enchanted kiss of a Rioch nymph again.

As the shouting behind us amplifies and the snaps and crashes of a forest pursuit sound through the forest, I may get to exact my revenge momentarily.

However, whatever is traveling through the forest is far louder than a nymph and coming from the side. Troll? I hope not. Nor would I be lucky to meet a bobcat when I'm flightless and still dizzy from the enchantment effects I experienced.

"Move higher," I yell to Willow in case it's a cat. She needs to be out of pouncing range.

Instead, she looks toward the west and settles her feet on the ground. She sighs. "It's not here for me." My mate rubs at her chest and keeps her eyes downcast.

And then I see it. Hellhound. It's a young one, yet still able to easily rip a fae limb from limb.

I launch myself forward, scoop up Willow, and attempt to tuck her between twigs of brush.

She yips and struggles, pushing away from me. "Stop."

"I must hide you." If she slides between the branches, I can turn them to stone, and she will be safe.

"They won't hurt me."

It's too late to find if that's true because the hellhound circles us, snarling. This is it. My demise and I couldn't even protect my mate for longer than a notch on the sundial.

Arms out, I hold Willow behind me. "I'm sorry. I wish we had more time."

The hellhound leaps.

Scrunching my eyes closed, I spin toward my mate, shielding her with my wings, hoping she may escape if it takes me first.

The strike doesn't come.

I blink, finding Willow pinned between me and a young elm, eyes wet. They're an aqueous blue color now, and I long for the chance to learn what the color shifts mean.

I thumb away an unseated tear from her cheek, and she turns her head, swiping away the moisture with her palm.

A heated charcoal and meat scented snort along my wing reminds me how close I am to death.

I glance back to find red-veined orange eyes. The pupil is a wide void from which my reflection stares back at me. I look exhausted, disheveled, thin, and my hair is far longer than it should be. This is not the mate I can be. But at least I still have all my limbs, though I'm not sure why. A diplomarian from the Enforcer Court met her doom from a hellhound at their territory's edge. The witnesses said they didn't even see the beast until it was on her, crunching away before she could scream.

Hellhounds don't pause.

Every bunched muscle shows beneath its nicked and scarred, pale skin. It snorts, moving my hair before it backs away, turns, and bounds back into the forest.

I exhale and drop my head forward, resting it against the bark close to my mate. Inhaling her scent calms the ache in my body and mind. Everything will be fine as long as she's with me.

CHAPTER EIGHT

TO SAFETY WE GO... FOR NOW

WILLOW

I have to get away from this Unseelie.

The uninterested hellhounds have offset my plan. My guess is because there are still a few more runes brutally carved into Kage's other wing. They must be protecting him and possibly keeping him locked in the forest, like the Unseelie believe. The wing he mutilated—that hurt him. How long will he take to heal from the damage of the carvings? I can't imagine what he's been through.

And I shouldn't care.

Damn these leaking eyes. I wipe my face and wiggle backwards, wincing at the tug on my wings.

"Are you hurt?" Kage's face holds genuine concern when he is so injured.

"Just pulled my wing a little on the bark."

He backs up in an instant and holds out a hand to me. "Turn. Let me see."

I can't take it. I can't touch him anymore and if he puts his hands on my wings… it's far too confusing.

Fluttering sideways, I put a few wingspans between us and brush off my gray smock. "We need to get to the bag for supplies and work our way toward the border."

There will be more hellhound run-ins, I'm sure of it. And danger from birds and ground predators if we're not where the hellhounds are. He's unable to fly, leaving him vulnerable. It will only take one fox to spot us for my plan to still work. The thought of that potential moment makes nausea rise in my throat and I rub the area to take my mind off it. I'm trapped by fate, not anything real. I need to be diligent in remembering that.

Kage tilts his head, watching me. He reties the silken sheet, and steps closer.

I dart back.

"Why do I scare you?"

The things I could say. *Because you're on the dark side of faeborn and took what was mine.* But also, *because you make me feel things I should not.*

And again, I'm saved from responding as a nymph gasps. She's a few trees from us.

I whip my magic out to backhand her into a gigantic oak.

Kage lifts his eyebrows. "You have power, my mate."

"No time." I run, staying on the ground because if one nymph found us, the others won't be far behind. They'll see me faster if I'm hovering. A shift of magic in a nearby tree has me growling. "The dryads may be communicating back to them."

"Understandable." Kage leaps in beside me, keeping my pace. "Do I smell like a nymph?"

"Would that help our escape?"

"No."

I glance his way. "Then why are we talking about this now?"

Voices to the east make me curse and divert our direction.

"Because I wish to make things as easy as possible for you to not fear me."

I roll my eyes. "Too late."

"What does that mean?" His voice is soothing for an Unseelie—not irrational or malicious, though I wish it were. The falsities he's hiding behind are as confusing as this damnable bond thrumming between us.

Shaking my head, I point to a rocky part of the landscape. "We can travel through there without being seen. We'll need to get the bag later."

Kage slows to a halt. "I'm going to need answers to many questions in order to help."

"We just need to run."

"Where, my flower?" He signals around the woods. "This is nymph territory. You think they won't find us as we run randomly toward the border? It will be days before we get there."

I only need his wings to heal or for him to slash the other runes first, even if the thought makes me nauseous. But then, it won't matter. The hellhounds will remember their enemy, and I'll be down a mate I don't want.

He sighs and narrows his eyes as he looks through the forest, then jogs toward a tree. He picks up a rock and a clover, holding it inches from the bark. "Pay attention." He's not talking to me, and a magical shimmer dots the bark in front of him.

We're standing in front of an occupied dryad's home.

"Have you ever attempted to escape a petrified tree?" Kage inhales, and the clover's soft green petals shift into stone. He throws it at the dryad's home tree, where it dents the bark, before clunking against the roots on the ground. "Try to get out of one made from stone."

I hold in a gasp. I shouldn't be surprised, and I'm not entirely angry about the threat to the dryads. They're sustained by the energy bond with their home tree, and typically honor peace and harmony in their forests, so I'm not sure why they've aligned themselves with these nymphs who capture and violate kings.

Kage points toward the path we ran from the nymphs. "We need coverage from our enemies. Preferably a hiding spot with water and a food source. Even an abandoned owl hole near a stream will suffice for now. And all dryads of this glade"—he glances around at the trees with a scowl—"will allow the nymphs who are hunting me to keep aimlessly wandering or this entire territory will be known as the Rioch Stone Forest. Do you understand?"

That was quite the threat aimed at the fae hiding in their trees. But Kage is a king. He takes what he wants, when he wants it, even though, in this case, he's demanding protection from a terrible situation he shouldn't be in.

Utter silence rolls through the trees like a reverse wave, and I fear there will be anger among all forest-kin directed at us, because with a threat like that? Can he deliver?

The sounds return, bringing back the slight breeze, tapping of branches, and the rustle of crisp leaves. Due west, the trees of a young, but thick, copse part.

Kage signals that direction. "Most excellent choice, my friends."

Chapter Nine

THE POWER OF A KING

KAGE

We make our way through brush that continues to become thicker and more difficult to navigate.

My mate silently follows me with a furrow painting her brow. Even if she won't admit it, the nymph's nauseating sweetness is on me, so she's bound to notice; though some Seelie senses are not as honed as mine. The details of situation I'm in remain cloudy, and I'm afraid as angry as I am about it now, I'll be far angrier when I understand all.

I'm part of something deceitful. My mate is a widow, and she came to save me, I think.

"Who sent you?" I ask.

Her eyes stay on the surroundings of tall grass and low brush. "Typhon."

That's a surprise. "Why? My brother knew where I was going."

Her lips firm, and she keeps her eyes on the ground as we pass through grass, now twice our height. Not being able to take flight is unnerving enough without knowing something is terribly off about why my mate is choosing now to be silent.

I stop and turn to her. "How long have I been here?"

She lifts her chin. "Is that something you truly want brought to light right now?"

Dread spirals in my chest. "I always wish for full understanding. It's the only way to plan the steps to make things right."

She snorts, as if that concept is ridiculous.

"Willow?"

Grabbing a nearby stalk, she plucks at a seed-head.

"Look at me, mate."

She storms past me.

I catch up in two strides and step in front of her.

She stops and backtracks.

My shoulders sink. "Tell me. How long?"

She meets my gaze, though her eyes are tired and vacant. "One moon under a full cycle."

My breath leaves me in a whoosh, and I fight to stay upright. I don't remember a moment of it until Willow. I've been away from my court, my family and friends for far too long. How much have things changed while I was under the spell of a nymph who was—nausea rises in my throat—*with me* frequently?

"Are you so glad I told you?" With a tight smile, she steps around me again.

I let her lead, needing time to take that in. I will rip Ornia from the inside out, and that will be the last moment I ever touch a nymph.

It grows dark as we follow the path the dryads provide for us. We scare a rabbit before the thick grass we navigate transitions to clipped-back patches from deer and their like.

My mate, a Seelie stranger, leads me along on legs of defined muscle. Her wings have delicate scrolling veins that shimmer in the moonlight. What does my brother know about her that I don't?

I take longer steps to get closer to her. "Why did he send you? You're extraordinary but—"

"You don't know that." She doesn't turn around or acknowledge me with anything but her answer.

"We had an instantaneous bond. That alone is extraordinary." Tales will be written about us, I have no doubt. When she picks up speed, I repeat, "Why, Willow?"

She spins so fast, I nearly run her over. "Because the nymphs had you trapped to breed you during the upcoming An Nasc Iontach." She grits her teeth, fists balled at her sides and her wings buzz as they flutter. "They threatened all Unseelie with instant death from the hellhounds if they crossed the Rioch borders, so Princess Ember called upon me, the spring faery widow, to rescue you so you didn't provide heirs who could claim the Crown Court under the nymph's agenda."

So many questions. I raise a finger. "Who's Princess Ember?"

"The princess of the Spring fae court and your brother's mate."

"Huh." I always thought Typhon would be the first to find his mate. Without the pressure of being termed king, he has a far easier time being social than I, and frequented beds regularly. I didn't predict him bonding with a Seelie, although I didn't see myself with one either, yet, here we are.

"She's kind?"

Willow appears utterly aghast. "Does that matter?"

"Yes. Is that not an obvious thing with Seelie?" They're in control of our territory and people in my absence. The Seelie princess better be kind.

Willow huffs and turns away from me.

I grab her hand without thought, then find myself sailing through the air and tumbling through the grass, courtesy of my mate's powerful magic. Laughing, I shake my head, push myself up, and readjust the sheet I'm covered with. "Apologies, mate. I wanted more information about you, and am inclined to touch you." Everywhere. Soft touches of learning. Gentle, then maybe not as gentle. Fingers skimming skin, then gripping—

She's already walking along the path again. "What could you possibly care to know?"

"Everything." I flap my wings and get the slightest push back onto the path. "How about the impressive power you have that doesn't seem to take any effort from you? That's an obvious reason to send you after me." Pride inflates my chest. How fortunate I am to have such a mate.

She shrugs, wings slowly fluttering as she stomps. "I still have some additional strength from the bond of my mate. My other..." She peeks back at me. "I could pose as someone getting over my grief and readying myself for intimacy again. I was the perfect choice." Tears well in her eyes.

I can't have that. I step in front of her, walking backwards as we go, pondering what form of comfort she needs.

She leaps forward to shove my chest. "And then you kissed me."

That makes me stop in my tracks. "I did?"

"Yes," she yells. "That is not what I wanted."

My chest squeezes. "You don't want me?"

"No. I didn't ask for this." She hugs herself.

If she wouldn't toss me to the skies, I'd wrap myself around her and hold her. It's all I want, but I can smell the nymph on me, and I already overstepped by kissing her. Wish I could remember that moment. I nod and turn. "I'll make myself worthy of you, mate."

"You are wrong about that."

I straighten. I can talk my way through any problem, if given the chance. The nymphs didn't allow me that courtesy and they'll pay for that, but my new mate? "Not to show arrogance, but I'm an Unseelie king."

She bares her teeth at me. "Exactly."

She's so angry. About being my mate? "Are you rejecting me?" The thought is impossible.

"Yes," she says, crossing her arms. She's serious. She can't lie.

Raising my eyebrows, I huff. "No."

Chapter Ten

THE PROBLEM WITH MATES

WILLOW

King Kage doesn't understand that I'll never truly be his, but I need to keep my mouth shut. He doesn't get to know more about me, and I certainly don't want to know more about him.

"What do you mean 'no?'" I blurt. Why did I do that? It doesn't matter what he thinks.

He studies me intently with a half-smile on his face. "You're not rejecting me."

The audacity. I raise a finger, getting ready to lay into this arrogant king, but the trees rustle too synchronously. I turn my back to the king and listen. *Chatter*. At least nymphs can't seem to keep their mouths shut. Not that I've done well at that either.

"You'll change your mind about me, mate." Kage wears a calm grin, though he should be running.

"Have the nymphs not harmed you enough? Go." I point to the path the dryads laid out for us.

His eyes narrow, reminding me of the monster within, but he aims his stare toward the voices and takes a step in that direction.

I grip his hand without thinking. The charge of energy is so pleasurable, it's terrifying.

But the contact pulls his attention. Too well. His face relaxes, eyes going half-lidded, as he stares at our entwined hands. Then he's closer, warm, tingling energy surging into me like a wall.

It's not until he touches my cheek that I realize his lips are a mere flit away from mine. I jerk away, trying not to show how quickly I'm breathing. I bet he can hear my heart pounding, though.

The Unseelie Grimm brothers enjoyed pointing that out as they escorted me to the Rioch border. *"You have the heart speed of a mouse. Are you terrified, little Seelie? Or turned on?"*

I'd been terrified—of the strength and intensity of the Unseelie warriors, and of being found out, or failing when I'd come so close to being able to find and end the king. I wish I were terrified now, but no, my heart is pounding a lustful beat and I'm having to pay close attention to my wings to keep them from buzzing.

Kage only licks his captivating lower lip, then bites it. "I mistook you staring at my lips as a need to have them against yours."

I don't respond. Can't actually, because there's no air in my lungs. With a spin, I follow the path, jogging.

Now is not the time to kiss me, not that there is a good time. I should have taken a lover long ago because the need to touch and be touched is overwhelming and inappropriate. But it was impossible to find someone who didn't treat me like shale. I'm not brittle, flaked, or cracked. I will not turn to dust if someone treats me as they would any other stone. In fact, I'm far harder than I was before.

Another rush of the wind urging us forward tells me we may be in trouble. I speed up.

Kage strides beside me. "Take to the air, mate."

"They may see."

"You're growing tired and I'm not sure how much farther the dryads will take us." He raises an eyebrow. "Or is your racing heart solely for me?"

"Ugh." I groan and lift off the ground. My legs are tired and cramping.

"Good. Keep going." Kage falls behind.

"What are you—"

He turns, crouches and slams both hands to the ground, unsettling a wave of energy. He backs away, watching as a blue light soars outward and away from us. Screams sound in the distance.

"What was that?"

Turning back, he resumes a casual jog. "A type of glamour. I feared they had a ward set against magic and didn't want that to injure you if—"

A crack of thunder silences him and the entire forest.

He growls. "Damn the guardians. Fly."

I do just that for seven flutters when the rain starts.

It doesn't begin as a gentle shower, though. It's an instant downpour of heavy, fast drops. They pound around me in warfare. One hits the tip of my left wing, sending me spinning. Another slams into my side, knocking the air from me. I pull up and fortunately land with some grace, tuck my wings and run toward the trees, ducking under what brush there is in the field.

Kage is on my heels.

Another drop smacks my shoulder, and I stumble, but am caught around the waist and righted, then released.

"Almost there." He raises his wings over us as we run, grunting every time he's pummeled with drops. I'm not sure how he's holding them up—the hit to my wing already feels bruised—though Unseelie wings seem to be uncharacteristically strong.

I press my palms against the closest oak tree and work my way around the bark until I'm under the area with the most coverage.

Kage stays behind me, shielding me.

"I'm fine." I turn, resting against the bark. "We're covered. Was that a reaction to whatever glamour you did?"

"No." His jaw is tight as he stands close, still covering us. Rain leaks between the spaces in his wings, and there's rage in my blood for his wounds. "I'd wager Ornia has discovered I'm gone and thinks that a rainstorm will either slow me down or make me return."

What pours from the skies seems less like rain and more like a waterfall. Even under protecting trees and Kage's body, we both grow soaked, making fabric cling to hips, thighs, and—

I startle when Kage's nose brushes mine.

He only moves back a breath this time, and his lips curve up in a sexy shape that makes my mouth dry. "Did I mistake the way you were eyeing my *sheet* for you needing me closer?"

I must be thirsty. And hungry. I wrinkle my nose, hating the ache inside me that needs to be filled.

Kage sighs and stands straighter, and I grow more irritated. Distance is what I need and what my body doesn't want.

He glances around, eyebrows lifting. "Stay here, mate." He attempts to arrange a fern so it covers me, but it's a silly act with how the rain drips down the grooves of bark, soaking my back and wings, and the hard drops blast into mist, drenching me everywhere else.

"Leave it be." I tuck wet strands of hair behind my ears.

He backs away and jogs, dodging drops by leaping under plants and leaves. Halting under a holly bush, he breaks off a few leaves, then walks to the edge of the bush and looks toward me. He makes a spinning motion with his hand.

I tilt my head. "Turn around?"

He nods, cracking the hard green leaves and plucking a close-by fuzzy grass seedpod.

"Why?"

He raises an eyebrow, faces the bush, then he pulls the sheet from his hips and drapes it over a branch.

And I'm left with a dropped jaw and an eyeful of muscular backside. It is, unfortunately, the best derriere I've ever seen in my existence. Round, yet firm, with two dents of muscle near his lower back. My mind fills in a vision of my legs wrapped around those hips while they thrust. No. No no no no—

"Mate?" Kage has his eyes narrowed and red as he stares at me from over his shoulder. "I'm going to bathe, then return to you, unless you don't stop looking at me like you want to bite my buttocks. Do you wish for me to return now?"

An embarrassing squeak leaves my dry throat and I clamp my hand over my mouth and turn, putting a hand on the tree to keep myself upright.

The rain and distance muffle Kage's dark chuckle, which is good. So good.

CHAPTER ELEVEN

NEED IS A GREEDY THING

KAGE

My mate is a blissful distraction, but I'm still full of rage and remorse. It threatens to bubble up and snap, but this isn't the time. My wings are a mess, and I have a mate to protect.

However, the more I think about what Ornia did, the harder I scrub my body with the hard almond-scented leaves and soft grass fluff. My skin is sore, and only when every inch of me is bright red do I stop. I'm tempted to leave the nymph's sheet hanging on the branch, but I don't believe walking about naked will help me woo my reluctant mate. Instead, I rinse it in the rain, which is easy to do since it's still steadily pouring, then wipe down my body, hoping the holly will replace any scent remaining on the silk.

The drops sting, and water is pooling. We won't be able to stay in this spot much longer, but it's hard to see anything of use in the downpour.

When I sprint back to my mate, she's still facing the tree, but her forehead rests on the scratchy bark, when she could rest against me.

"You're tired." I press my palms to the tree on either side of her.

"I'm thirsty," she whispers, unmoving.

I run my knuckles between her tucked wings, over the ties of the clinging, coarse fabric.

She's smaller than I would have guessed under the smock. Perhaps she meant to portray herself as shapeless, and the wicked rain thwarted her plan. I'm glad for it. She lets me touch the dent of her spine, but presses closer to the tree when I caress the flare of her hips.

I put my hands back on the bark. "Then drink."

She looks back at me, almost shyly, peeking down, then fully facing me when she realizes I've covered my cock. "I'll get a leaf to fill?"

"No need." I bend my extended wing, channeling water to my shoulder so that it catches on my collarbone and runs over my chest and down. "Plenty here, mate."

She surprises me by leaning forward, opening her lips against my chest. Her eyes, blazing purple, hold mine until she swallows and lets them flutter closed. When I release a pleased purr in my throat, they flash open, and she moves back.

I lean closer. "So jumpy, my mate." I recreate the water stream. I want her lips all over me. "Here. Again."

"What was that? The sound you made?"

"The Unseelie hum of pleasure. I enjoy providing what you need, and having you take it."

Her lips part again to drink against my skin. She takes four gulps, then looks up at me.

I dip, holding her gaze as I slowly move toward her lips. What excuse will I give this time? The flush running up her neck told me to move closer? I'll say her eyes pleaded with me to push her further—to take what's mine.

She doesn't bolt when I pause a mere whisper from her mouth. Her expressive eyes crinkle, creating a tortured crease between her brows before she lifts.

The press of her lips is a shock, but I fight my needs, digging my fingertips into soft bark instead of sweet skin, and kiss her back. Magic swirls within, tightening around my soul. The most perfect scent opens my mind to everything that can be, and when she moans, parting her lips, my tongue is there to gather her flavor.

"No," she whines, pulling back. She darts out from under my arm. "No. Damn the gods, no. No!" Her last word is a screamed whimper.

I follow her into the pounding rain. The water gathers halfway up my calves. "Willow?"

She takes hit after hit of the raindrops but moves back when I try to cover her. "This isn't how my fate was supposed to go."

"Fate is not predictable," I yell over the loud hiss of the downpour. "It only is."

"But you're..." She shakes her head, eyes bloodshot and a darker purple. "You're not supposed to be mine." Sucking in a hard breath, she presses her palms against her temples and whimpers.

My eyes widen. "Liar's curse." I snag her into my arms as she collapses. "Say the truth, mate. Say I'm meant to be yours."

"No. It can't be..." She grits her teeth in agony, and while I respect determination, this is over the line.

Panic replaces all the pleasure humming in my blood. "It is. Even you believe it to be true. I am yours, Willow, and you are mine. You must say it."

"I... won't. I'd rather die."

Chapter Twelve

LYING IS A HUGE PAIN

WILLOW

So, this is how I leave this world.

The sensation of the liar's curse is five lightning-struck daggers plunging into different sections of my brain. It crushes my lungs and heart. I wish I understood who made the gods curse us. It's beyond unfair to be called out in this way. It's intolerable that I can't make the truth untrue.

"Tell me why you'd choose this." Kage's voice somehow eases the pain. Why does he have to be mine?

I shake my head, but he grips my jaw. I want to panic, but damn him, he makes more pain ease away.

"Say I'm yours." His eyes are violently red. "Willow, you must tell the truth." He sounds so honest—so sure. As if him being my fated one is the easiest thing in his life when it is the hardest in mine. "Why won't you, my flower? Why deny what is exactly as it should be?"

"Because you're Unseelie," I gasp out. "You murder. You ruin... everything."

His brows furrow, and the pain is too much. I really may die from this agony. I need to sleep. It might help.

I'm jostled into opening my eyes. "Why do you say that? What happened?"

"My mate," I growl, tucking my face against Kage's chest, "is gone because of you."

"Your past mate?" Kage presses his cheek against mine, pinning me between his chest and face. He's so warm as he cocoons us in his wings. "How?"

I can barely hold a thought with death blooming within. I shake my head.

"Explain. I swear to you, Willow, no Unseelie would harm another without reason, especially me." He sounds so angry. "Undo the curse. If you don't, I'm going to lie too and we'll both be fully wrecked." His whisper is so pleading and distant. "Say it, please."

I would laugh if I could breathe. I am weak. Sucking in as much air as I can, I whisper, "You're supposed to be mine."

The slicing of my insides instantly dulls. It calms degree by degree until I'm left withered in Kage's arms, feeling like my mind has oozed out of my head.

"Good, my mate. We'll figure things out together."

I want to kick him. Punch. Bite, and then tell him that nothing will make me care for him, but my body refuses to move, and my mind isn't on my side, because his scent mixed with the almond of the holly bush seems to be the only thing I can grasp on to and want near me.

I close my eyes and let him hold me. Maybe he'll have mercy and toss me into the rising water.

CHAPTER THIRTEEN

THE MOST VICIOUS MATE

KAGE

Willow goes boneless in my arms.

I pry open her eyelid. Her eyes are now sunny-sky blue and vacant but surrounded mostly by white. No burst vessels or impending death. She's just in a deep sleep.

The rain somehow increases and neither of us will survive this if we don't get to higher ground. I position Willow over my shoulder, raising my wings to take the brunt of the punishing drops. Running is hard in knee deep water, but I do the best I can, getting to a deeper part of the grouping of trees we're in. There, I stand on elevated roots, looking for anything that may help us survive.

My eye catches a shadow on a tree trunk, and I run down the root and back into the water for a better view. "That's it."

The old tree is half dead with a wide-open chasm leading to a hollowed out inside. I sprint for it, wading waist deep through water that carries leaves and conifer needles and... a half rotten berry. I snap my attention to where the water is flowing and find a sprawling berry bush with several ripe berries still attached.

"Was that intentional?" I ask the trees, grinning at the lack of response. No dryads are here at the moment. They're probably focused on keeping their home trees' roots grounded and worrying about the surrounding plant and animal life. Have they lived through a nymph tantrum before? "Let's get settled in, mate."

I work slowly toward the shadowy opening, sliding around the side in case there is wildlife holed up from the storm. The scent of fox, squirrel, and bird is faint and old, but there are bats. Not a problem. I head in and sigh at the instant relief of not having my wings pummeled with rain. It takes a moment for my eyes to adjust to the darkness, but once they do, I find open, dry space with twisting inner roots, down feathers, bone, and fur. Paradise for an Unseelie needing harbor in enemy territory.

"Alright, mate. Let's climb." I follow twisting roots, working upwards in case any ground animals decide to return. I miss my wings beyond measure. They ache from the weight of rain and blood from reopened cuts.

There's a deep space between four old roots that I can both stand in and cross with five steps. There's even a small, vacated nest. I have a plan for that, but my remaining energy needs to be used for one more thing before I deplete it.

I slide Willow down my chest, and hold her, memorizing the way she fits in my arms and hoping she'll let me experience it again when she's conscious and not hating me. We may not know much about each other yet, but she'll learn to talk to me. I'll find out about her past mate and how to make things right with her if I were at fault, though

I truly doubt I am. I'm eager for her to share more with me. Carefully lying her on the root next to the nest, I sweep the soaked red locks off her face. "I'll have patience with you, Willow, and hope you do the same for me."

She scrunches up in a ball, hiding her face against her fists. I need to move fast in case she wakes.

I run down the roots, extending my wings and gliding haphazardly to land too hard on the dirt floor. When I head back into the pounding rain, the groundwater is even higher. I'm tempted to return to the nymph's coven only to make more of their territory into mud. Take out their supplies and huts and let them fight among themselves for tree hollow housing.

Flapping my damaged wings helps drag me out of the highest water, though I get a few good raindrop smacks to the head for using them for something other than protection. Fortunately, the berry bush is close. Dashing under it, I tuck my wings close so they don't catch on any thorns, and pull the fabric from my hips to gather berries.

The tug in my chest from being parted from my mate is extraordinary. So many of us hope to find one specifically meant for us, or one we appreciate enough to create a bond that will grow. Few can say their bond sparked to life like a late summer wildfire, though. How fortunate for me. If only she didn't seem to despise me.

I eat as much as I collect before dashing back into the cave, using my wings to keep from being taken away by the rushing water.

After I gather a handful of rabbit fur leftover from a past predator's meal, I drag myself up the roots. Willow still sleeps, though she's turned to her stomach and has her arm stretched out as if seeking me... or a weapon to murder me with. Who knows?

I unwrap the berries, placing them in a clean nook the roots provide, hang the silken sheet so it will dry, and take inventory of what else our shelter needs. With the fistful of rabbit fur, I grip the nest of prickly twigs and channel my magic from one to the other.

The ones in my kingdom who know of my powers keep quiet for fear that others may try to take advantage. When you can turn the component of one thing to another, fae get ideas about turning wood and stone into gold and gems, as my father did. But the brilliance of fate included a safeguard. My spells only last so long.

The stone clover I created to show off for the dryad and secure us a route to safety will only stay stone for a mere quarter moon cycle. Then it will break into pebbles. Then dust. By the full moon, only ash will remain.

Father was so angry to find his new room of ruby and diamond, turned dull and gray and gone. I was such a failure to him. He didn't realize my other strengths. Though he didn't plan to die or for me to lead the war against the Sidhe in his honor, either. I don't have a clue whether he'd have found pride in me or would still consider my gifts to be trickery instead of power.

As I reposition my mate on a bed of rabbit fur instead of bumpy wood, she makes a quiet moan that must be pleasure, and I'm thankful for my rare, though temporary, magic. It's exactly as it should be.

"Sleep well, queen. When the rain ends, we will go home."

I gather a little fur and make myself a softer patch of root on the other side of our makeshift room as exhaustion settles in. My eyes are drooping when my mate lifts herself up from the fur bed.

"Willow?" I push up to my elbow and drape a sore wing over my naked hips.

She mumbles nonsensically, but I catch a few slurred words like, "cold, wet, and strangling." She tugs at her gray tunic, getting on her knees and pulling it off entirely, throwing it in my direction.

I sit up. I should take it, squeeze out the water and hang it to dry, but I'm too busy devouring my mate's body with my gaze. The taut dip between her hips and stomach makes my fingers twitch to grip that slender spot, and her breasts are small, perked up with dark nipples. I suck my tongue, wishing my mouth was all over her. Who knew Seelie were so enchanting? Similar, but so different. Her wings cast a dewy shimmer over her backside. I want to bask in that shimmer, see how it flows over me as well.

Except, she can't stand me. Or, from what happened with the liar's curse, she's in denial of wanting me.

She blinks drunkenly, like she can't quite gain her bearings. "Kage?"

My heart may beat out of my chest. "I'm here, my flower."

Her wings buzz and my mate—my mate that doesn't like me—drops to all fours and crawls to me.

Chapter Fourteen

THE WAKE UP

WILLOW

I wake stretched out over the warmest body that smells like sweet, merciful—I blink and gasp, pushing myself up so fast, a dull ache in my mind reminds me of the pain I experienced. Wincing, I settle back against my ma—Kage.

There was a kiss and then... the memory is fuzzy because the agony slicing through my mind had taken most of my focus, but bits of our conversation sweeps in as I meet Kage's calm green eyes. He swore he wouldn't kill without a reason.

"What would my mate have done that deserved death?" I ask.

Kage purses his lips and raises an eyebrow. "That's what we're starting with this morning? Not that we're out of the flood, and I have breakfast, or that you're most certainly naked on top of me, and I'm also naked?"

I'm tucked under his least-injured wing, which is warm over my backside.

I gasp and flail off him, sending dust and tufts of brown fur floating about. When I hit a wall, I crouch, trying to hide behind my hair. "How dare you."

"Oh, it wasn't me, my flower." His eyes trail over me in the dim light of... wherever we are. "You mumbled something about being wet and then you stripped." He bites his lip with a—yeah, that's a fang. "You called my name and crawled to me."

"I wouldn't—"

He pushes himself up, raising a finger. "No more lying. You did."

I can't help looking over him. Little light trails into the space we're in, but I can see well enough to note his light hair is dry and mussed, cascading over his bare chest and stomach.

"What happened between us?" I don't want to know, and yet I do.

"I went against every instinct I had and held you while we slept."

I huff. Why would the same fae who killed my mate choose restraint with me? "That's all? Are you leaving things out?"

He raises an eyebrow. "Things like how my heart nearly exploded when you curled into me and pressed your fucking perfect nipples against my chest? Or how I laid in agony because I understand I scare you and, for now, you don't trust me?" His lips curl into a smile, showing both fangs. "How it was still the best sleep I've ever had? Those kinds of things?"

"Yes." I attempt to clear the deep rasp from my voice. "That's all that happened?"

"It is." He tips his head toward a root. "Want a berry?"

My stomach growls, and I go to stand, but I'm naked. "Where's my dress?"

He points to a wet heap on the ground. "You were in my arms before I could hang it up, and I wasn't about to move you."

My face is hot, and I rub my cheeks. Covering myself as well as I can with my hair, I forgo my typical grace and crouch-walk to a cache of dark berries.

Kage chuckles. "Are all Seelie so shy?"

"No." I think back to the last Springfest Sprint. "My kind wears many thin silks to highlight their shapes."

"You don't." He nods toward the soggy pile of scratchy cloth.

"It's a mourning garb." I wave him off before he can comment with vitriol or pity. "No, my kind are not typically shy. The princess of my court enjoyed being publicly claimed by your brother."

"And you watched this?"

"I was a referee for the event." When he doesn't seem to understand what that entails, I nod. "Yes. Only to make sure there was no infringement on the rules of our traditions."

Settling back against the feathers on the ground, Kage lifts an eyebrow. "So, my brother took a mate by following her traditions."

I shake my head. "He followed your traditions as well. At least, that's what his second said."

"Donovan was there?"

"He was."

Kage hums. "What traditions did Typhon follow?"

Is this an Unseelie test? I wish it were lighter in this place so I could see Kage's eyes better. "Why should it matter to a Seelie what your traditions are?"

"Because we will need to follow them as well, so when we return to our court, our people accept you as queen."

CHAPTER FIFTEEN

WHAT HE LEFT BEHIND

WILLOW

I choke on my mouthful of berry.

Kage goes to stand, but I wave him off. He tilts his head. "I understand that what happened between us was unexpected, but because I'm a king, you will be queen."

My laugh pitches high and trill. "I'm no queen."

Kage hums. "Not until we meet the traditions. Until then, what are you?"

"I'm a widow." I expect that to land hard. For him to lose his patience with me and maybe even lash out like he should. I'm prepared to fly to safety, though from the sound of the rain, my only option is to hover within this... tree. It is a tree we're inside.

He shrugs. "I was once a prince, and now I am a king. Our paths change through our existence. You may be a widow, but now you are also a mate, and you will be a queen."

"Kage," I groan.

"Yes, my flower?" He does not play fair. He should hate me; despise being tied to someone who doesn't want him... the thought tightens my chest. Fine, I want him, but only because of mystical involvement. He smiles like he sees my internal dilemma. "What traditions does your kind have for matehood?"

And now would be another brilliant moment to lie if I could do such a thing. "It's not as complicated as yours."

"I wouldn't call ours complicated, only strategic in making sure both partners wish to be entangled." His voice is practically a purr when he mentions entanglement. "Willow?"

"Hm?" The berry is delicious, and I appreciate what he's done for me so far, but I cannot forget the past and move on. What about the future I should have had?

"I have a confession."

That gets my interest. "And what's that?"

"I know about your matehood traditions and am happy to oblige. I also know about the Springfest Sprint, the Winter Court's Snow-in, and an enticing, secretive event called the Evening of Glamours."

My jaw drops. "How?"

"It's required of me to understand all types in our world. I've met kings and queens of each fae species. We talk."

"You kill."

His eyes narrow, but I don't see red. "Only with a principled reason. We're not able to move past this, so tell me what happened with your previous mate."

"You sentenced him to death, and then you and your kind murdered him."

"How?"

I'm taken aback by his direct question and scowl at him with his inquiring expression—raised eyebrows, lushly pursed lips, and tilted head.

"Focus, my flower. Though I'd be happy to delay our conversation if you need to keep your lips busy in ways that don't involve talking."

I can't even say I don't want that. My mouth waters for another kiss. I shake that feeling off. "He was going to visit a cousin for a few days on the summer fae border within their territory. While traveling, Unseelie took him and brought him to you." I can tell he doesn't believe me by the twist of his lips. I nod. "It's true. The queen, like every other fae—except the Bogeyman—cannot lie."

"The Bogeyman can lie?"

I forget how much he's missed since being held prisoner by the Nymphs. From what I understand, Auralia and Kage were close, even though she's now bonded with Donovan and imprisoned within the Crown Court. Hearing about her deception from being tangled up with the Bogeyman may make him wander into the rain to get back to his castle. I should want that, but I need answers. And the ache in my chest when I think of him being pummeled by rain and swept away would annoy me more if it actually happened.

"One story at a time." I chew the last of the berry and grab the sheet hanging over a twig, wrapping it around myself. It smells like him. His warm skin... What were we talking about? Ah, yes, we went off topic. "One of your guardians came to our queen to inform her you had taken my mate at the Nameless Pass. You claimed he was trespassing and decided that was grounds for execution. His things were returned to me for confirmation of his passing."

Kage's eyes squint. "That's exactly what she said? Word-for-word?"

"Yes." I grab my wet dress and twist the fabric to squeeze out any remaining water, then hang it where the sheet had been. "She said there was no use in fighting what had happened. Your kind would only annihilate us." I look him over as well as I can in the dim light.

He's deadly power, though calmly lounging as he listens intently to me. He shouldn't be so beautiful, but he is as he watches my every move, arm up and under his head, bunching his defined arm muscles. "And you felt the bond detach?"

Cheeks heating, I shake my head.

"I will question the Spring Court Queen."

I put my hands on my hips. "Why?"

"Because no one attacked him within Nameless Pass. Like Goddess Lake and Harmony Plains, it's a safe zone for all fae by warded blood pact. No blood shed, and no stealing of fae. It's why it's used for goods exchange and meet ups." He blows out a long breath. "And will be used by Unseelie for future meetups with all nymph covens." He swipes at his lips like the thought of them repulses him. Good. It does me as well.

Is that true about the pass? There has never been another beyond the Bogeyman with the ability to lie, and even if there were, Kage isn't one. I can tell by his reactions to the nymphs, this journey, and his conversations with me. But that still leaves questions as to why the queen could tell me such things. And what happened to Flint?

I let my bottom lip pop out from between my teeth. "I didn't know that."

Kage nods. "It's not common knowledge. If someone harmed your previous mate inside the pass, it would have pulled the ward strings to guardians from every race. When someone seems to have disappeared from a safe location, they were doing something wrong in a territory they shouldn't have been in and no one wants to talk about it." He holds up a finger. "Or they wanted to disappear, and no one knows about it."

"That's not possible." It's not. Right? "Why would he do that?"

Kage remains quiet, sending my thoughts spinning.

It's possible my mate was where he shouldn't have been. He… wandered. But if he had left me and our home willingly? That hurts quite a bit. Sure, fae can't lie, but it's not like I was questioning Flint's every whereabout when he stayed away sometimes. A deep, cruel inner voice tells me I was afraid of his answer.

I always loved him more than he loved me.

Chapter Sixteen

With the Gentlest Touch

Kage

"Answer me," Willow says, words choked. "Why would someone want to disappear?"

Our conversation has saddened my mate, and I bring my wings in tighter, pinning my hands to keep from reaching for her, because she's going to need to come to this conclusion on her own. Kings are often targets for blame. We lead, so we take on responsibility for our people. If I come forth with pure denial, she'll only see me throwing around my title or trying to win her with deception. I'm not, though I do want to win her over.

"I do not have insights into your past mate's mind, Willow."

"But why would someone leave?" She's so close to a new consideration, but I must be cautious.

"When did he go? And when did your queen hear from this guardian?" That is a mystery. The queen must have been told the untruth to be able to relay it to Willow, though she'd have known it wasn't entirely true.

Her jaw tightens. "Three cycles ago. Almost four."

I blow out a long breath.

"What?"

"You're not ready to hear, my flower." I don't wish her pain, however, there's no avoiding it if she continues on this path.

"Tell me," she pleads.

"Willow." I shake my head.

And that's how I learn my mate is quicker and stronger than she looks. She smacks into me, forearm against my throat as she presses me backward against the ground. "Tell me."

"Fine." Gripping her wrist, I pull her trembling fingers up to my lips so I can kiss them. "I haven't taken a life in over a decade, and that was a war."

Her wings buzz, and her lips go firm. "You're ly—"

I stop her words with my lips but pull away just as quickly. "No. More. Lies. Think about it, mate. Untruths are not in my vocabulary, and you know it."

"Well, they're not in the queen's either," Willow says, voice trembling. She's so warm against me, and the closeness is making me hard, but this is more important than my dick.

I shift, moving up to my elbows as she straddles my stomach. "Consider her exact words. And now, mine. I did not kill your past mate. I did not order harm to him or know of his existence until you accused me of doing such a despicable thing." I point at my temple. "Feeling fine."

Her glare softens. "Why would she tell me that? How?"

"I'd like to find that out as well."

She gives a sharp nod, re-tucks the sheet, points toward the cavern of our tree haven, and flies up where I can't follow.

I flop back and blow out a long breath. I wish I had Auralia to talk to about this. My second is undoubtedly bossing around my brother and the rest of the castle in my absence, but I could use her advice. She's always level-headed; always there for me with the exact answer I need.

After a while, I climb down the inner vines and wander to the soaked ground close to the mouth of our hollow escape. The rain has calmed, but it flooded the land. Willow will have to get berries when it stops, because there's no way I could cross without taking a swim back toward the coven, though that is still tempting. Would it be possible to turn Ornia to rain in poetic irony? The foul, false queen could be an experiment to see if my power works on living creatures. No matter what, she'll pay long before she can entrap another An Nasc Iontach partner, if that's her plan.

When the temperature drops, I head back inside. I'm surprised to find my mate sitting on the ledge of the upper hideaway, as if waiting for me. Her hair is wet, so maybe she needed a moment in the rain as well. Her eyes turn purple and her lips slightly part as I climb towards her.

I sit next to her because that's what my body calls for. We're tethered, and without touch and closeness, I'm not sure what the bond will do, but I doubt it will wander off.

Her frown grows tighter. "I can't—" She wrinkles her nose. "You're—"

When she remains silent, I lean closer, draping a wing over my nakedness. "You can't speak to someone so handsome, and I'm making you tongue tied?" Now is inopportune for humor, but I need more from her—information that is real and workable. Something to tie us further together.

Her gaze remains on the empty space in our hollowed-out retreat, but her lips tilt up. I want her eyes on me so badly, I can't help running a finger over her bare knee.

Her smile drops, and she swallows, but doesn't flail backwards. *Progress*. "I find it hard to trust, and this—" she signals between us, glancing my way. "This between us was unexpected."

"Yes. But also incredibly real. I won't betray you, mate. You'll find through time and practice that you may freely speak because it's my duty to protect you, my friends, and my kingdom."

There's a softness to her gaze I haven't seen before. "Friends? Back at your court?"

"Yes. But my mate comes first. Please, tell me what you're thinking. I long for it." I've said "please" four times in my life—when my mother was dying, I asked the lady of the lake to spare her, and when she denied me, I begged my mother not to leave us. Looking back on it, that was a cruel request. And when Willow refused to tell the truth to end the torture of the liar's curse, and now, when I wish my mate, who doesn't want me, will give me something I can use to make her understand I am hers and did not wrong her in the past.

Willow looks at her fidgeting fingers. "Flint was my friend until his parents made a bet with mine and lost. He bonded with me, mystically, to repay the debt. I loved him, but..." She swallows and my mouth waters to kiss her throat. "Not all matches are perfect at first. He had regrets and stopped talking to me or seeking me out in the evenings. He needed time. *We* needed time to adjust. I was a superb mate. But he didn't see that before Unseelie took him from me..." Her eyebrows scrunch. "Or so I had thought."

I suck in my lips. Oh, the things I'd like to say. Not all fae are honorable. By nature, most of us are tricksters who love a diversion or a way to win a favor. I never knew this Flint Seelie, but he was not honorable, nor was his family. He hurt my mate. I'm glad he's gone, though that cruel trickster part of me wishes I'd have met her in front of him just to experience our bond smashing apart their previous unnatural relationship. *Mine.* But that is not a feasible thing. The only option now is to move forward and prove that what happened between us is the right path by design.

"You think I'm foolish," Willow says, twisting her fingers in the sheet covering her.

"I think you're relentlessly loyal, and you were in love." That sits hard in my chest, but the past is merely a stepping stone to the future, not the island my mate has refused to leave.

"He could have..." She swallows hard again. She is learning not to lie to herself and I'm glad she's realizing the words I'm positive she's said a thousand times in her head are not the right ones.

I turn and reach for her, unable to help it. Resting my fingers on her knee, I slide higher so my hand cups her skin. I want to harness her jittery energy if she'll let me.

"Have you ever been in love?" Her gaze follows the path of my touch.

"I love my brother, my friends. But as for romance, I thought I was at two points in my life. One was unrequited..." I leave that hanging in case she'd like to pick up that we're more similar than she believes. "The other loved me as well, but she and her family sought higher means for her, thinking I'd never be king."

Willow's eyes widen. "Is she still around? In the court, I mean?"

I smirk and move my hand higher, growing hard at the lean muscle of her thigh. "Jealous, my flower?"

She glares, but there's an enticing flush highlighting her cheeks.

"I'll take your silence as yes, but you have nothing to fear. Not only is she bonded to the King of the Hillock Court, I only seek my true mate."

Her eyes turn a vivid purple, and her scent blooms, making my mouth water. She bites her lip.

I reach up to tug it from her teeth. "Come here."

Her brows furrow, but she leans closer. "This doesn't—" Her nose scrunches.

Before I touch my lips to hers, I whisper, "This means everything."

CHAPTER SEVENTEEN

THE ABSURDITY OF WANTS AND NEEDS

WILLOW

He is not what I should want, though I'm desperate for him. He's also not what I should need, and yet, his lips pressed to mine fill up a chasm in my soul that will cave in if he stops. I never want him to stop.

Shame on me. Shame on my weaknesses, wants and needs and—

Kage's purring sound vibrates into my bones, and when I groan, his tongue touches mine. I haven't kissed much, but I bet my mate has because his skill is enchanting. The thought of him with others—nymphs and Unseelie—sends jealously sliding through my veins. I grip the silky strands of his hair and squeeze.

He leans into my tug, parting his lips in a blissful groan.

I tighten my fist, wanting to push every line to either get to know this Unseelie or have him end me just so I'll understand his mind more. "If I demanded that you may never be involved with another, what would you do?"

His eyes open, but halfway. "Intimately?"

"Yes."

"Who would I be intimate with when my mate is you?"

I glare, tightening my grip further, but that only seems to make him grin, which lands heat between my legs like I've never felt before. "Don't evade. I've seen your kind when it comes to mates. The spring princess has fallen into bed with multiple Unseelie, along with your brother. You all share."

"And you don't want to share me?" His lips curve up, showing the tips of his fangs.

Flexing my jaw is probably a clear sign that I'm struggling with this, but he leans a little closer and flicks his eyebrows as he waits me out.

I move my gaze to the side and mumble, "No."

"Little louder, my flower."

I turn a glare on him. "No."

He slides his hand up my thigh until he's cupping my backside, then drags me into his lap. "No, what?"

When I refuse to answer, he runs his nose up my neck, making me startle. His grip leaves me as I move away from him, flitting into the freedom of open air, giving me space I don't want.

Why him and me? Why is this union so painfully enticing? It shouldn't feel right to be touched by him. Yet it does and goes beyond that. His hands on me are necessary.

"Damn the gods for this." I flutter forward, wrapping my arms around him as the sheet slips away and his blazingly warm skin lights up mine. When I press my lips to his, he opens them for me, devouring my quick breaths. His kiss gives me a full-body hum.

"Bless the gods for this," he whispers, swirling his fingers against the sensitive place between my wing roots and cupping the back of my head with the other. He shifts and tucks his wings as he turns, taking me with him and settling me on my back beneath him. His eyes blaze red. "You must tell me if you need space, because I intend to give you none."

"What if he's not dead? And..." That makes me oddly sick and I can't pinpoint why. "He returns for me." I run my hands over the hard plane of Kage's chest. His collarbones are more pronounced with the darkness and, while part of me fears his dark form, my soul tells me his intensity is only because of his lust for me.

"What would you do?" he grumbles.

"I don't know. That's why I asked you."

He huffs a laugh. "And you want me to answer?"

I nod.

He growls. His kiss is desperate and deep. Then he's gone, trailing kisses over my jaw until he whispers in my ear. "I would tell him I might actually kill him if he returns, then I'd drag you off to our bedroom and show you, again, exactly why fate stoked our bond with such fury." He raises an eyebrow.

"That is more enticing than it should be."

"Good. Because you're mine, my flower." The rasp of his words lands right between my legs.

I suck in a breath as he reaches my neck. "Don't bite me."

He goes still, lifting his head and parting his lips from my pulse.

"The intimacy of your kind is brutal, Kage."

He trails his tongue up my neck, and I lift my chin. He hums and moves down. "One day, my flower. You will beg me to taste you here."

Chapter Eighteen

THE BEST EXPLORATION

KAGE

I want to bite my mate. Claim her. Experience every delicious inch of her that is mine.

But I'm king because of my restraint and diplomacy. My patience. So, while the Unseelie side of me is coming apart at the seams, I, the king, will treat my darling, reluctant mate like the Seelie she is.

The pairing isn't something I'd expect, though fate loves to trick the tricksters, and if my mate is correct and the An Nasc Iontach is upon us, it could create unlikely pairings between an array of fae. I'm not angry about it. Especially as my brother has landed in a similar match. It must mean our species are destined to coexist closer than we've ever been. If we have children, what would they be like? Perhaps the gods think it is time to combine our strengths and help us remember our weaknesses as they prep us for a prophecy on the horizon. Or perhaps they only wish to experiment to see what delights we would create.

I nuzzle back against my mate's neck, placing gentle kisses as she tenses. "I swore I would not until you want me to." That doesn't stop me from licking her throat and imagining sliding my fangs into her to complete a bond that's already so tight.

She gasps, and her hips lift, pressing the slick heat of her against my thigh. "Kage."

"Yes, my flower?" I give her neck a lingering, open kiss, and move down to between her breasts. Devouring another has never been on my mind during intimacy, and yet I want to touch, taste, and tease every inch of her. I wish to consume her until we are one.

"What are we doing?"

I shift my thigh forward, pressing hard between her legs, and grin at the way she arches. "It's not obvious?"

"Not—" She gasps when I draw a circle around her nipple with my tongue. "This doesn't feel real. It's a dream or an enchantment."

"Some have called fate the ultimate enchantress." I learn the shape, tautness, and texture of my mate's nipple with my mouth, and she makes the most delightful whimper. Am I being cruel to tease her when she still has so many concerns? Maybe. "Do you wish to wake up?" I skim her puckered flesh with my teeth and fangs.

Her guttural groan is music, but she remains tense.

I give her other breast attention with fervor, then push up, caging her under me. My cock lies heavy on her hip. I'm positive my eyes are violently red and Unseelie shadows paint every dip of my bone and muscle, making me look like danger and death. "Do you trust me, my mate?" I settle clawed fingers over her heart. "Does your soul recognize mine and understand I'd never harm you?"

Her jaw tightens and for a moment I think she may twirl out from under me, as she's so good at doing. But she touches my cock with soft fingers, wrapping them around me, and thumbing the head, slick with need. "Yes."

I study—memorize—her face like this, centered in her flames of wild curls. Her lips are pursed sin and I want nothing more than to make them red and puffed with kisses, then see them wrapped around my cock. But that's another day. One when she's not confused or reticent about us.

I nod, closing my eyes against the intense pleasure from her delicate touch. "Good." I drag claws up her chest and neck, tilting her chin so I can explore her mouth.

"Why do they feel good?" she asks.

"What?"

"Your...claws." She swallows. When she gets comfortable with me, accepts my body with full trust, we may never leave our bed.

"They're not as sharp as you thought, are they?"

She shakes her head. "Can they scratch me?"

"Only if I'm too rough with you." I drop my head to brush my lips over hers. "I won't be, though."

"Your fangs are sharper." It's not a question. She's noted the difference.

"Yes. Unseelie use each as weapons when needed, and pleasure when wanted."

Her wings buzz, and she crinkles her nose.

"And what was that for?" I ask, raising an eyebrow.

She purses her lips and looks past me.

"You won't tell me, mate?"

She answers with a sigh.

I bet I can get her to tell me. I run my claws over her thighs.

She spreads for me.

The temptation to enter her is overwhelming, but so is the need to savor and learn. "I'm very persuasive, you know." I slide down onto her, making sure our bodies touch as much as possible. "What makes my mate's wings buzz? It's happened a few times now." I kiss her shoulders, then run my fangs over the soft curve.

Buzz. It's brief, but she has them pinned under her as she bites her lips as if holding in a smile.

"So silent now when she was so full of questions before." I crawl backward, nearing the edge of the dropoff, delighted that she seems not only comfortable with my lips and claws, but she's lifting her hips to me and writhing. "Too frightened of me to say?" I dip my tongue into her belly button and grin at her gasp. "Or are you scared of how much you want me?"

"Kage," she growls, trying to move away, though not aggressively.

I can't have that. Not with the scent of her passion so thick in the air.

"Both?" I dig my claws into her thighs to pin them and lick her dripping pussy.

She sucks in a breath.

"Fuck, Willow. You taste like rain-soaked honeysuckle."

She laughs, then moans as I spear her entrance with my tongue.

I press my thumbs to both sides of her slit and part her so I can see and lick deeper.

"I'm going to…" She's up on her elbows, looking at me with confusion.

I swirl my tongue around her clit. "… tell me what makes your wings buzz?"

She jabs her foot into my side. "Don't stop."

"Is it pleasurable? Will that make them hum?" I lick and purr.

"Goddess." Her legs tighten in my grip, and she falls backward.

"Is it, mate? Do your wings buzz when you hear something that makes this stunning pussy clench?" I thrust my tongue as deep into her as possible.

"Stop talking." My saucy mate is endlessly amusing.

"I will when you tell me."

"Yes, damn you. Yes. It's when something excites or angers me beyond reason."

I hum and purr as I kiss her clit. "And you're angry about it?"

"A little." She's so adorably grumpy.

"What a good mate. Now it will be easier to give you pleasure."

I let her thighs go, grip her breast with my claws, and slip a finger into her pussy, knowing she feels the sharp slide in her tight channel. I graze my fangs along her swollen folds, grinning at her whimper and the pulsing buzz of her wings.

She's ready.

My pulse kicks up as I sense how close she is to coming apart for me. I surround her clit with my lips and suck.

CHAPTER NINETEEN

LOVE TO FEAR YOU

WILLOW

I shouldn't enjoy this. Kicking Kage away comes to mind, though that falls away because I can't hurt him, and I don't want him to topple over the root we're on and stop what he's doing to me. I also shouldn't be rocking my hips against his face, yet here I am, submitted to him and the magic of his mouth and—blessed be—his claws and fangs. Those should not ignite passion in me.

But damn me, they do. I hate that my blood heats, and while I may curse the fates, I've never been so cared for in all my days. His attention is all on me, and my pleasure.

He isn't taking me as I expected him to when I so clearly offered myself—he was supposed to mount and complete, not caring whether I'd experienced a twinge of pleasure.

Though that thought is flimsy and cracking with his Unseelie claws piercing my backside and the one that's slowly rubbing inside me in a way I'd never in an eon expected to feel right.

I swallow the lump in my throat—the past seems distant and shaky with this fae's hands on me. This may only be a fateful enchantment, but I want my mate. "Kage," I whisper as my insides tense.

"Yes, my flower?" He licks me like he's waited to taste me forever.

My heart expands, my soul reaching for his. "Don't stop."

"Never, my queen." He purrs and thrusts his finger inside me, then closes his lips around my—

I swear my end must be upon me as the strongest pleasure drags me under in sharp pulses. Every muscle seizes. When my body calms, I'm altered. Even further enchanted.

But now is when he'll pounce. My muscles tighten, but not in pleasure. I prepare myself for a violent claiming like Typhon did with Ember, and what I've accidentally witnessed between Donovan and Auralia, though they all seemed to enjoy that. I'm not Ember, and I'm certainly not Auralia.

Kage wraps an arm under me, then rolls, dragging me on top of him as he settles on his back. He wraps his wings around me, cocooning me in warmth. His manhood is solid against my hip, and I gulp as the lustful ache reignites between my legs. I've never known a need so defiant it's a sickness. I shift my hips closer, trying to line us up. We need to get this over with. When he's done, I'll understand what to expect in the future.

Claws send a pleasing tingle over my neck and jaw as Kage lifts my face. "What are you doing, mate?"

"You need release." I try to slide off him and get into position.

His wings tuck tighter around me, pinning me on top of him. "Later." A dark tint has settled around his red eyes and the hollows of his cheeks, his collarbones, and everywhere there is a dip of muscle.

He looks so… beautiful. And calm. It makes no sense. He makes no sense.

I furrow my brows. He's already given me pleasure. Why does he care for what I want? "I don't understand."

He furrows his brows right back at me. "Do you want me? Would it please you to give me release?"

Would it? "Why are you asking?"

"Your mood shifted." He sucks in a long breath and drags me upright as he sits up. "Did you not enjoy that as much as I did or do you feel obligated?" There is an even deeper glint of danger in his eyes and his voice is a terrifying growl, though the orgasm is preventing me from fearing him. The amazing orgasm I deeply enjoyed.

"Should I not?"

He tilts his head. "Bringing you pleasure was the highlight of my existence, and while I'd be a troll to not want to sink into the sweetness I was just exploring, I'd do myself a great injustice to allow my mate to service me like a—"

"Nymph?" I smile. My heart beats a little faster when he turns his glare back to amusement. "I'm not a nymph. I don't have the curves for that, nor the ability to adjust my size."

"I enjoy your size, but"—he unwraps his wings from me—"I'd rather stop this right now than have you not completely want what we do together. I want to savor you, not rush through while ignoring your reluctance." He signals to the little setup we're hiding in—the berries and pile of fur. "Go, mate. Enjoy other things."

There are few things as clarifying as being offered exactly what you need, but don't want.

"I want to enjoy you, but..." I push up, hiding my nudity with my hair.

Kage sweeps my curls back over my shoulder and drags the claw of his thumb around my breast. "But?"

Closing my eyes, I attempt to focus on what he asked as he sends more tingles of pleasure over my skin. "Your kind violently claim each other."

He hums. "Some Unseelie are more *passionate* in their movements than others, as I'm sure Seelie are as well."

"And how are you?"

He shrugs. "We'll have to see exactly how well fate matched us."

I nod and shift to line us up again, but he runs his hands down my sides. His closeness is warmer than any other. It's so easy to crave him, to be intrigued by his features. My fingers seem to raise of their own accord, and I halt a wing's width from his cheek.

His lips tip up and he leans into my touch, eyes closing. Somehow, he trusts me, even when he shouldn't. I'm not someone any Unseelie should trust, and yet, they do. I slide my fingertips over the shadows that mean danger. He's so sculpted and perfect, it's emotionally choking, bringing a knot to my throat.

I run my tongue over the perfect lines of his lips, which part on a sigh.

He flaps his wings, sending dust and fuzz fluttering around the cave as he pushes himself up and carries me with him over to the pile of fur. "I'm excited to introduce you to our bed," he says, dropping to his knees, then turning to lean against the wall of roots. "This is not what you deserve." He takes my face in both hands and when I gasp, his tongue touches mine.

I melt into the deep kiss, holding his wrists to keep his hands on me. Straddling him, I squeeze his hips with my knees.

"Ride me, mate." Kage's voice is a pained growl against my lips. "When you're ready. And only if you want me."

I'm not ready for what any of this means, but I'm powerless to resist him.

Kage can't seem to touch me enough as he maps my stomach and hips, then brushes the sensitive place between my legs with his thumb.

I tighten my grip on his shoulders and moan.

He licks his lips. "You like my fingers."

I huff a laugh as I roll my hips against his touch. "Yes." I grip his cock. "Do you like my fingers as well?"

"Mate," he whispers. "You are unlike anything I could have imagined."

"There's a wild amount of truth to that." I guide him to my center and sink the tiniest amount. He's huge. The head of his cock isn't in, and yet, I'm full. "You won't fit."

His shoulder is taut under my grip. "I will."

I shake my head, trying to sink a little more.

"Willow, look at me."

Panting, I blink open my eyes.

"Do you want me to fit?"

"Do you?" Maybe we shouldn't be doing this. It's a sign, a glimpse outside of the enchantment. He should be concerned about what he wants.

"Of course, I do. I'd have been inside you the moment I found you, but that would not have done well for us. I know you better now. This will be better. So, do you want me?"

"Yes," I nearly scream. I sink a little lower, but I'm afraid of hurting him if I push for more.

Kage grips my chin and turns my head. He kisses my neck, moving up to whisper in my ear. "Say it, my flower. Tell me you want my cock to fill you completely."

The tightness of passion tenses between my legs, and my wings buzz, making Kage chuckle. "I...I want you to fill me completely."

"Yes, my mate." He kisses me, gripping my hips and moving me up and down on the tip of his manhood at a slow, rhythmic pace.

My legs shake, and I want something more. Something different. I want him all over me, consuming me, in me, and... I shrug and pull at his shoulder.

Fortunately, he understands what I can't seem to voice. He lifts, taking me with him as he turns, guides my legs around his hips and kisses me, teasing my entrance in shallow thrusts. He kisses me with slow sweetness, moving a little deeper, then retreating. Has he practiced this—opening up a lover on their first time?

And that makes me wish I had fangs. Claws too. I dig my nails into his backside.

He bares his fangs. "Does my flower want more?"

"Kage."

"Yes?"

I growl and dig in more, and he thrusts in.

When I cry out, he gently kisses my lower lip. "How's that?"

Gentling my nails, I bring one leg up higher, opening further. "More."

His smile is light and makes any tension in my chest melt away. How could any fae be this beautiful? His hair, even with a few tangles, is warm in color, and as shiny as he is. Every sharp angle, each sparkle in his red eyes blends to make one breathtaking male.

But that's not what makes me most warm, most unarmed, when I'm still not sure I should do this. It's that I *want* to do this. Actually, I can't imagine not being here, locked as close as we can be.

He's inside me, holding still so I adjust to the size that I wasn't sure I could physically take. He's so... gentle.

I run my hands over his hard backside.

I don't understand this fated tie between us, but for now, I don't need to. I just need this... whatever it is.

Chapter Twenty

A Future of Stinging Pleasure

KAGE

My soul may explode with joy. I'm figuring out my mate. If she's still scared of me, it's not because of my appearance or the intensity I'm sure pours off me as her tightness stretches around my cock.

She wants more.

I bet she never asked her past mate for more, or if she did, it wasn't because she wanted it. She'd wanted to *please him*. To make him want her when I was existing out there all along, not knowing my mate was destined for me, but in a terrible forced bond.

Our time together will be matched and happy.

I slide my nose against hers and give a teasing lick to her lips. "I'll give you anything you want. Tell me what you need."

A sheen of sweat makes her hair stick to her face as she nods.

Brushing the strands away, I bask in the warmth of being this close to her. She's so lovely. The furrow has disappeared from between her brows and her body has relaxed little by little. I want her to be melted with bliss. I want her to be mine completely, with us both knowing we can experience this whenever, however we want, as long as we're together.

I move slowly, picking up the rhythm of her shifting hips. "You like my cock inside you, don't you?"

Her eyes flutter half-closed. "Am I that obvious?"

Kissing her cheeks, I nod. "You're so slick for me. And I'm so hard for you. There is nothing better than this, Willow."

She moves impatiently under me, sinking her fingers into my hair. "I'm close, I think."

I purr and her wings hum back. "Let's make sure you know. Do you want to come?" I carefully sweep my fangs over her jaw, gather her closer with one arm, tilting her hips up.

"Yes." She opens more, letting me press in deeper at a different angle.

I watch her face for pain, but she gasps from pleasure, biting her lip and wrapping her arms around me until she's clinging to my neck with one, and pressing a palm between my wings.

That spot makes my cock swell. That is a pleasure point we clearly have in common. When I did the same to her, I thought she might orgasm on the spot. I'll explore that another time when I'm not dying to be close to her. A time when I can tease her for hours in our warm castle. In our bed.

I hold her to me as I thrust. "Too much?"

She shakes her head, and I return to devouring her lips and stealing her gasps, returning several moans of my own. Every moment of friction sends sweeping pleasure through me. Her scent is a pleasure.

The slide of her hands as she explores me... there is no word that could measure what that feels like. She must know that our match goes beyond fate.

She arches, muscles tight, grits her teeth, and whimpers.

I grind down onto her. "Let loose, my flower. Give it to me."

"Fuck," she cries out, clawing at me. When I drive deep into her, she bites down on my shoulder, and her channel squeezes me so hard.

There's no holding back from losing all control over my hips, and I'm coming. Hot pulses from my orgasm are nearly secondary to the pulses of magic flowing through me to her and back again.

Muscles weak, it's all I can do to keep upright and not crush my mate, so I turn to my back.

She clings to me, sprawling across my chest and keeping my softening cock nestled in her pussy. Our breathing evens out in the tree's quiet, and I'm perfectly warm, my blood humming with euphoria.

She runs her fingertips over the tiny indents she left on my skin, before moving to my chest, seemingly to learn me instead of aimless wandering. When she gets to circling my nipple, my cock twitches.

Giggling, she lifts, but the furrow returns. "Will it always be like that?"

I stroke her cheek with the back of my fingers, wonder-struck at the beautiful flush. "We'll have to keep trying to find out." I'm sated, and yet hardening again.

She cups my face, and it's the strongest victory of my life. Trust, pleasure and even a bit of obsession lie within her touch. At least I hope it does.

I wish to know everything about Willow, to fix everything she's had to overcome if it's still bothering her. I only hope she feels similarly.

I slide in and out of her body, entranced by the way we fit, the tight pressure, yet soft sensuality between us. "Are you ready for me to court you, my queen?"

She opens her mouth, closes it, twists her lips, and sighs. "We're already out of order."

I raise an eyebrow. "So, you know the courting ways of my kind, then?"

"I do."

"Good. So, when we are within the safety of our keep, I want you to say that when I formally court you."

Her eyebrows raise. "Truly?"

"Yes. The phrasing doesn't have to be exact, only the intention."

She gives a pursed lip grin, and I can't wait to understand every one of her expressions. "This is something you want? Me?"

"Very much so. Does being a queen bother you?"

"Not as much as…"

"What is it?" I grip her hips and roll us so she's under me again.

"It's very foolish to tell you how full of hate my heart has been. How I'm still struggling with the truth I feel and the confusion of what I'd thought to be true."

Humming, I turn so we're both on our sides, facing each other.

She keeps her leg wrapped over my hip, bringing me endless joy.

I nuzzle her hair and swipe my thumb over her soft cheek. "Understandable. It was quite sudden. But you're not foolish. And we will figure out exactly what occurred to what's-his-name."

She glares until I make her eyes roll back by raking my claws over her thigh.

"Chastise me later, mate. This is of the utmost importance." I press deep into her, earning me the prettiest moaning gasp, and watch my cock disappear inside of her. "Look at you taking me so well. Mm. Does my queen like me deep?"

She arches closer, her wings buzzing as if trying to escape her. "Yes."

I slowly slide in and out of her, tickling every nerve in my lower half. "Wait until I fuck you on top of silks in our candlelit room. Wax will drip so perfectly down these gorgeous breasts." I lick her nipple.

"Wax?" she asks, sinking her fingers back into my hair. I can't wait to trim and oil my strands so she can see how much better my mane is than the mess it's become. She teases her nails over my skull.

My neck prickles, and I exhale with pleasure.

Her gaze shoots to my mouth—my fangs. It's hard to keep quiet about how we'll play with those, too.

"Wax. Yes." I even sound like a demon to myself. Gently, I rake my claws up her side, and swirl them around her breast. "It will sting with heat." I squeeze and sink my cock deeper when she writhes. "And pleasure."

Her pussy squeezes as she cries out.

I grit my teeth and fight the pull to release. Not yet.

She drops her hands back to the fur bed and sighs, cheeks flushed and shiny from the pleasured effort of working our bodies together.

"You're game for playing with wax, then?"

She laughs the prettiest tinkling note. "You have such interesting ideas, mate."

The warmth in my chest swells and magic swirls within me. "So, I'm your mate? No more ideas of rejection?"

Her smile drifts away, and she strokes my cheek. "I'm willing to explore this, along with the past. It's the only way I'll be able to move forward with my life."

Our life. I settle onto her fully, wrapping her legs over my hips and slowly thrusting. "I, Kage Brightline Jenderos, King of the Unseelie Crown Court, accept."

CHAPTER TWENTY-ONE

THE PAST PLAN COMES BACK TO BITE

WILLOW

Unable to help myself, I slide from the cocoon of Kage's wings, and sample the dips and valleys of the muscles along his stomach with my tongue.

The rain stopped yesterday evening, but we haven't. Though I'm not as sore or tired as I thought I'd be. It has to be the bond, because I've barely eaten.

My tie to Flint wasn't like this. We were magically bound with herbs and magic. We were locked in, but... it was settled. I'd asked another bride moons later what her bond was like and she beamed, telling me her soul continued to grow, to entwine, with her mate's. I'd hoped for that, but Flint and my bond was just there, not bright or warm or urgent.

I'm still struggling with the past and the control fate has me locked in.

But the way Kage looks at me—the way he blinks open his eyes now, watching me trailing my tongue over his hip, and smiling with every inch of his beautiful face like there's no one else that could ever pleasure him like I do... I don't care if it's fate. I want this feeling to never go away.

And maybe I could see myself with him, in the castle of Unseelie that are so unlike the Spring fae I'm accustomed to. I could join the loud buzz of them. The brashness. They're so chaotic at dinners and behind bedroom doors—if they bother to close them.

But Kage wouldn't let anyone hurt me. A harmless fly buzzed through the tree yesterday, then came after the berry I was eating. My mate removed the non-existent threat as if the insect had been a hornet coming for my blood. And yet, he doesn't seem to do it because we're bonded. It's as if he's built to protect. We're not as unalike as I'd assumed.

While my previous bond wasn't a fated snap into place, there should have been more to Flint and me. A spark of passion and an inkling of respect would have been a fraction of what this fated bond means to me.

Shame on me for believing I could merely wish love into existence.

Not that what I have with Kage is love. Though I wouldn't speak that out loud.

After the pain I'm positive will remain in my memories forever, I will only speak the truth about my relationship with my mate. I don't know him well enough to understand if he will accept me fully. This enthrallment may only be destined for a short time, because it's too good. It's too easy to be with him. I may as well test the boundaries before I get too deep.

"I won't share you," I whisper, taking his length in my hand.

He raises an eyebrow. "No?"

I shake my head and kiss the base of his hardening manhood. "No. If we're doing this, you're mine alone. I can't be with another who would leave me wondering what I'd done wrong to be left in the cold each night."

His smirk becomes fangy, and he reaches to stroke my cheek. "I don't want to spend a single night away from you."

"I hope that doesn't change." I let spittle drool from my tongue to the head of his cock and swirl it around with my thumb.

"It won't. Not ever." The gaze he gives me is red heat. "Fuck, Willow. You're so good at that. Take me."

I guess we're good for now. Time and location will tell if that changes. I lick my smiling lips and do as he asks.

He drops his head back as he moans, then pops up again as if he can't miss any move I make. I have an Unseelie king under me; watching me like I rule him. Pride swells in my chest and lust heats between my legs. I can't help myself. I reach down to stroke the ache.

Kage's red eyes track my movements, and his lips part, showing his fangs.

Too much? He might not like that. I pull my hand back up.

"Willow," he grumbles. "Don't you dare stop. Make yourself feel good."

This must be an enchantment. I ache. I reach down to play with my wet, swollen channel, gasping around him and losing focus as pleasure crashes into me.

"Fuck." He delicately threads his clawed hands into my hair. "Look how pretty you are when you come."

My wings buzz, and the moment I remember to suck him, he curses and releases soaking heat into my mouth. I take all of it into me, wanting others to smell him on me. It's mine. He's mine.

My family will hate this, and will probably hate me more, but it's time I stopped seeking love that's never been there.

He stretches out his wings. The daylight stretches over the soft gray membrane—the soft, gray, *flawless* membrane. No words or symbols. No runes that are both grounding and protecting him.

My lust freezes over. "Your wings."

He raises his eyebrows. His fascinating claws recede when he stretches his fingers and examines his healed skin, wincing at a few points. "Still sensitive."

"Can you fly?"

He unwinds from me, and steps to the edge of the root room, then gives a testing flap. "Ow. Not yet, but it appears matehood is healthy for me."

My stomach does a lurch. Healthy until he meets the wandering hellhound, or the nymphs that will gladly mark him again. What if they're surrounding us, ready to strike, and that's why the rain and flooding have stopped? Our mate bond has only crippled him more. Healed him enough to put him in danger, but not enough to get him out of here and to the safety of his court.

And to think, this was exactly what I wanted. I still need the truth about my past mate from the Spring Fae Queen, if only for peace of mind, but I've also discovered I don't want to be without Kage. I don't care if he's Unseelie, or a king.

Flint never wanted me, and Kage does. I feel it, see it—by the goddess—I taste it in the desperate way he kisses me. Yes, fate captured us, but there was a reason for that.

I can't lose him. What's the rest of my life worth if it's not lived with those who care for me?

"Mate?" Kage drops in front of me, pulling me close. "I can feel your panic."

Wait. We still can leave. I push him away and stand. "I have to get to the bag."

"The supplies you talked about while we were on the run?"

"Yes." I gather my gray dress. Putting on the mourning garb is phony, but it's all I have. "There's an item that can get us out of here if we're very lucky. Stay here."

"I go where you go, mate."

I turn and press my hand to his chest. "No."

He raises his eyebrows. "You're serious?"

"You must stay hidden." I lean to look over his wings. "The hellhounds will find you."

"And what if they find you?"

"They don't care about me. I'm Seelie. But you? They can't find you or..." I shake my head. The thought of what I used to want makes my stomach sour and heavy.

"Willow. I can't let you just wander into nymph territory on your own. We go together."

I take a step back from him. "No, we don't. They won't harm me. They will come directly for you, and your court needs you."

"*Our* court." His brows furrow, but his eyes remain their pure, stunning green.

I wince. There's so much I've been keeping from him. Not maliciously, but because I wasn't sure how he'd take the news of everything going on back at his keep, and I didn't want him barreling away—at first toward escape, and then to protect him. Instead, we've spent these two days wrapped in passion, speaking of ourselves or silently contemplating the swirl of magic whenever our eyes meet. Those things were more pressing, and now, there are consequences of putting very real and dire conversations off.

"A lot has happened since the nymphs detained you. And once we're to safety, we'll speak of it." Or he'll be dropped into the situation, and I won't have to explain a thing.

"Willow?" he says my name as an unamused question. It's nearly a shock that I've grown so used to his calm demeanor, and yet I don't fear his intensity as I would have days ago.

"And if I don't return, go to the Northern border. The gentry of the Enforcer Court and his second in command are there, seeking and dismantling wards while awaiting your return."

"The Grimm brothers are involved?" he asks over a growl. It makes sense. They're the deadliest members of the Enforcer Court and seem to gather more respect than the king and queen from the conversations I've overheard.

"They're safe on the outskirts, but if you come with me, we will cross the hellhounds. Without the runes on your wings, I doubt you'll have protection from them. It will take seconds for them to..." I choke on the words, swallow the lump in my throat, and shake out my tight fists. "There's already too much to think about when it comes to you. Don't make me lose you before we begin."

He lifts me, cupping my head and pulling me in for a searing kiss.

I cling to him, arms and legs tightly banded around his body.

"Willow." He presses his forehead to mine and magic swirls up between us, asking for release.

"I won't be long."

"That is true, because I'll be with you."

CHAPTER TWENTY-TWO

A MATE SO DECEPTIVE

KAGE

For a Spring Seelie, my mate can get downright icy when she wants.

She stiffens in my arms, leaning back to glare at me. "You will stay here."

"I will not." There is not a chance that I will let my mate run near the nymph coven without me there to guard her. Plus, it would give me an opportunity to get more well-deserved revenge.

"Kage."

"Willow." I grin. "You ready?"

"No."

I kiss her forehead once more, step back and grab the sheet, wrapping it around my waist. "Well, get ready, my flower. We have nymphs to battle and hellhounds to avoid."

"Kage. I can be back quickly. Do not follow me."

I shrug. "Who said I'm following you? I can take us near the nymph coven and you can guide us to where you left the bag. What is in there, anyway?"

"An amulet to call your brother. He was trying to get you out, but the nymphs warded the territory against him. I think that was tied to the runes on your wings and since they're gone..."

"He can suck us through the Earth and back home with his magic. Brilliant." I put pep in my step as I walk down the root to the base floor of our refuge.

Willow's wings buzz, and she drops in front of me, putting her hands on my chest. "The hellhounds will kill you."

"You don't know that."

"I do." Her eyes are wild yet pleading. Her lips firm, and she pushes off my chest. "That was my plan—to get you out of the coven so they could eat you. You're no match for them. It's why the nymphs brought them here. Your kind is a mere snack and now you have no protection."

"You're only trying to anger me into not going with you." And she is angering me. She wasn't happy with me at first, but to forge a plan to feed me to the hellhounds? That's unsettling. "Do you still wish me dead?"

"No." She shakes her head and swallows as she rubs right below her throat. "But Kage, I'm telling you, there's more to this than you understand. Lose the pride or you won't ever return to your kingdom, and they need you. Auralia needs you."

Tension tightens my spine. "What happened to Auralia?"

"Promise me you won't follow me as I get the satchel. I will tell you as soon as I return."

"No. Again, I'm going to lead."

Stepping back, she crosses her arms. "Then you'll never know what happened because I won't tell you, and you'll be dead."

"Mate," I grumble. "Tell me what happened."

"Swear not to follow me."

I get ready to do that, because I can make my way to the area she's headed without her help, but she raises a finger. "Or get any closer to the nymph coven. Swear it, and I'll tell you everything."

I flex my jaw. "Do not ask that of me, mate. I will protect you with every breath I have. Why would you make me swear against that?"

Her wings droop. "I cannot put you into any situation that would end your life or imprison you. I won't let them have you because of your stubbornness."

"Says she who is showing a remarkable amount of stubbornness this very moment."

Willow nods. "You need to let me do this. After, I promise to tell you everything."

My head might explode. Has my mate figured out my deep need to know everything about a situation so I can fix it? Clearly. "Why would you withhold this information?"

Her expression is more like resignation than apology. As if she's still on her own. "For the same reason I do everything. To protect. I said nothing at first because I didn't want you to escape before harm befell you. If you'd have known what's happened, you'd have walked through the flood to get back and been captured again, or killed."

"As if I can't take care of myself?" I yell, pointing at my chest. "As if I haven't seen war and resolved a thousand conflicts?"

She takes a big step toward me and matches my volume. "As if you wouldn't jump in front of a hellhound, an arrow, or a flood to protect me?"

Of course I would. It would take no thought.

She sets her palm against my chest. "Fae become stupid when it comes to mates. Trust me. This is the safest option. I'll be fast. Far faster without you."

I hate that she's right. "This is not fair."

"It's not. I will go to great lengths to protect what is mine."

Oh. This is not the power struggle it seems like. It's her declaration to me. Her promise.

I drop my crossed-arm stance and step against my mate, pulling her against me. She melds into me, made to fit me precisely. "And if I don't agree?"

"I will fly so high, you won't be able to track me if you try." She kisses my chest and blinks up at me. "And if you still follow, I'll knock you senseless with a rock, drag you back here and leave you unconscious while I run this errand."

"Fuck." I grip Willow's chin and kiss her.

When we're both breathless, I nod. "I swear not to follow you unless I hear you scream, or feel the tug of your panic, or we get to dusk. If that happens, I'm coming after you."

She nods. "It won't take me that long, especially when I'm flying."

I flap my wings, barely lifting off, before I flinch at my stinging skin and drop back to the ground. It may be a moon before I can use them properly. "When you return, we're also going to talk about you withholding needed information to get your way."

"Okay." Sucking her lips between her teeth, she steps toward the exit of our hollow tree. "I will understand if you do not want to see me once you've returned to your keep."

I turn my back to her, hands on my hips as I fight to process the information.

"I never want to hurt you, Kage. But I will to protect you."

Dammit. How can I stay furious when she speaks such sweet truths.

I slowly turn, but the mouth of the tree is empty.

My mate has started a dangerous journey without me, for me.

CHAPTER TWENTY-THREE

WAY DOWN

WILLOW

I must calm down. If Kage thinks I'm panicking because I've encountered trouble, he won't be bound by his promise to stay safely tucked in the tree. Part of me wishes that would happen because a flutter out of the cave had me understanding what longing means.

I thought I had felt need before Kage. I thought I'd been in love. How wrong I was. Enchantment or fate, whether cycles or days, my entire life altered entirely when he touched me. I see things so differently now, which is a reason I need him safe, no matter how he treats me afterwards.

He is mine, and I will do everything to protect him, because that's the type of mate I am. He will either accept that, or he won't.

I wrinkle my nose and land in the nook of a tall elm, catching my breath. What will I do if he doesn't accept me? Spend another handful of cycles pining for someone who's not there for me? Thoughts of Flint are still there, but my discovery of a portion of the truth has dulled the sparkling image I had of him. I'd like to know what happened to him, but my soul is well aware that his fate is no longer entwined with mine.

After my heart and lungs calm, and I focus my every sense on my surroundings to make sure I'm alone in my journey, I leap from the upper branch and zoom toward the tree where I stashed the satchel.

It's a relief to be wary of a nearby flock of birds, and I smile when I have to roll through the air to avoid colliding with a dragonfly. It's a day like any other. Maybe the hellhounds left the territory for good.

But my nerves catch up with me when I'm two trees from the hiding spot. What if they're stealing Kage right now? He's a king that can't fly. Can a hellhound take down a tree? What about two hellhounds?

I search the area, shaking those thoughts from my brain. Common forest sounds abound. There are still puddles from the nymph's anger storm, but they're ripe with movement from water skipping bugs and frogs who are loving the territory's watery expansion.

Can it be this easy?

I fly to the next tree, going as far as closing my eyes to sharpen my attention on scents. Unfortunately, nymphs smell like their forest, but hellhounds do not. There's nothing unusual here, though any close-by dryads can probably hear my pulse. If they can, they're still staying quiet. Fair enough. I wouldn't count on them to help the mate of the King who threatened them.

Branch by branch, I work my way to the small notch halfway down the trunk. There are no traps I can see. I even crumble a leaf and sprinkle it toward the dip in the bark, but nothing diverts or explodes.

"Okay, then," I whisper. Blowing out a breath, I reach into the shadows and sigh when I touch the fabric pouch. I pull it from the tree, and, when no one jumps out at me, I flip open the flap, then scream at the eight glassy black eyes staring back at me.

The small spider crouches deeper into the pouch as it hurtles toward the forest floor.

"Goddess alive." I dive. When I land next to the bag, I flip it open and leap back. Nothing happens, so I growl and move forward to give it a kick.

The spider stumbles out, fortunately, away from me. One leg is angled wrong. I shake my head. At least he has seven others. I'd apologize, but my panic might be bad enough to alert Kage. I gather the bag, peeking in to make sure the green amulet is there and no more tagalongs are present, sling it over my shoulder, then leap into the air.

I listen for hellhounds, nymph chatter, and my mate as I backtrack the path I came. We can be back at the Unseelie Crown Court by nightfall. But will Kage ever speak to me again? Withholding information he needed wasn't right, but I'm not regretting it. At least, as long as he's safe.

When the copse of trees come into view, I fly faster. There's no shouting or growling. Nothing seems amiss. Could it have been that easy?

Kage is there, right at the entrance, looking about as sour as any Unseelie can. Still beautiful, but extremely unhappy. Until he sees me.

He drops his crossed-arm stance. "Will—"

I'm plunged into water.

Chapter Twenty-Four

THE CRUSH

WILLOW

When I scream, bubbles trail out of my mouth. Inhaling is difficult, but I manage. Then something crashes into my left side, knocking me into a liquid whirlwind. Salt burns my eyes and I slam them shut, covering my face with my hands. I'm in the ocean?

Wait. This isn't right. It's a glamour. Nothing hit me. I hit the ground.

I blink, trying to clear my vision, but whichever fae is casting has incredible skills to build this false world.

"Kage?" I scream, but it's a warbled sound and bubbles. I gasp again, swearing water gushes down my throat, but it's not real. The mind is capable of incredible belief under the right lie, and since fae can only speak the truth, so many of us have honed our skill of deception in other ways.

I keep my eyes closed, though the motion of riding on a wave persists. I flail to touch anything other than water, but my limbs are heavy and slow. Enough of this. I ball my fists and punch my power outward. Even if I hit Kage, he's probably in this as well and could use a good exit out of it.

A few muted yips reach my ears.

Yes, this is a glamour. I haven't been transported to the ocean. I send my power out again, this time with a swipe. Grass and dirt tickle my palms when the world around me stops floating. After hacking false water out of my lungs, I sharply inhale, blink open my eyes and look up. And up some more.

My magic was probably a small thump to the human-sized nymph squatting in front of me.

"Move and I will pluck your wings off," she says, dark eyes focused on me. She's far bigger than a troll, the largest thing I've ever been around. It would take her nothing to complete her threat.

Other nymphs closer to my size surround us, some with bows and arrows, though no one points their weapons in our direction. They're merely holding them as if I'm no threat at all.

"Willow." Kage crawls closer to me, heaving like I am.

"Kage." I hate the panic in my voice, but it can't be helped. I try to move closer to him, but my body isn't working right yet.

"King Kage, am I to understand you had a mate when you came to me?" the nymph asks.

Kage ignores her and keeps on his path.

I try to close the distance between us, but my body refuses to wake from the dream state it was thrust into, then out of. My head hurts. I try to shift forward and flop. There's nothing broken, but the satchel tugs over my shoulder. We have a ticket out of this place if I can get to Kage. I seek the amulet in the bag, though my fingers aren't cooperating. But I finally find the smooth stone and hold tight.

"I asked if you had a mate when you were fucking me."

Kage bares his teeth in a malicious grin and pushes himself upright. "Ornia, your jealousy is showing in front of your nymphs. Though they're not really yours, are they? Nor am I and will never be." He has a rock fisted in his fingers. He truly would turn her into a stone statue, wouldn't he? If anyone deserves that fate, it is she.

"What are you hinting at, King?"

He chuckles and stands up with effort, one leg at a time.

I struggle to flop forward, though the nausea is leaving, and my fingers grow stronger with the amulet in hand. "Kage," I whisper. "Come on."

He takes a step toward me. "You're no queen, Ornia. Just a regular nymph with a princess complex that's far bigger than you are right now."

The crowd surrounding us shifts and whispers.

Ornia's peach complexion goes wildly red. "I asked you a question." The loudness of her yell is deafening, and even her nymphs cover their ears and cower.

Kage barely flinches. He wrinkles his nose. "Don't you know a queen should be strong, but fair at all times?" He takes another step toward me. "I suppose not, since you've treated me the way you did. That was the least queenly decision I've ever seen, and your coven will realize that soon enough."

The first line of nymphs shift on their feet, some closer together as they whisper, and some backward as if they're ready to run.

Ornia sneers. "Oh, King...you will pay heavily for your misbehavior."

"And you, normal nymph Ornia, will suffer immeasurably along with anyone associated with you."

The nymphs' chatter increases, and I see what he's doing. He's going to start a war among them as a diversion.

I hope Typhon is ready to pull us through the earth. By the time we get back, the nymphs will be tearing down this fake queen and fighting over who will rule them. My mate is smart.

I flex my muscles to get them to remember they are strong; not wobbly and weak. As I get to my feet, I flutter my wings, but Ornia grabs me.

She tightens her fingers so I'm locked into them and I'm back to not being able to breathe well. "You're not going anywhere. In fact"—she pulls me up just as Kage reaches for me—"you owe me a favor."

My jaw tightens as tension fills my chest. What ridiculous debt will she ask me for? I gave her an open door, a treat for a power-hungry fae.

She lifts her other hand and whispers to the orange jewel hanging from a golden chain that she's gripped in her fingertips. It looks tiny compared to her size, though it's about the size of the calling amulet. "Come."

The calling amulet. There're two? Or perhaps more. A divine gift that often ends up with royalty.

"Don't hurt him." That's all I can think to say. Please don't give me what I originally wanted Kage's fate to be. Don't let me get this far, this close, just to watch him be devoured.

"He is far too valuable to be fed to a hellhound, little springy." Her grin is frightfully huge, and it becomes apparent that I would easily fit in her mouth while she's in this form. "You, however..."

"Ornia," Kage yells, running toward her.

She laughs and backs away as a few nymphs step between him and the monster that carries me. "Halt and listen to me or I will feed this tasty treat to my pups."

I scent them before I see them. Smoke and brimstone burn my nostrils as they silently crawl like ghostly skinned beasts from between trees. Their growl is more terrifying than any glamour because these creatures are very real, and severely dangerous.

Ornia giggles and squats again. "What would you do to keep her, King?"

He moves forward, smacking a knocked arrow away from his chest just to have another replace it. "Let her go."

"You are terrible at following the rules." She squeezes me until I whimper and my back pops. I fight to keep from crying out.

Kage freezes in his tracks. "Stop, Ornia."

"What would you do?"

"I would stay."

I want to yell, "no," but this has to be some kind of plan.

"Would you? For this wiry-haired widow?" She glares at me. "Are you really a widow?"

I ignore her, afraid of speaking because I'm no longer entirely sure Flint is gone from this world.

"Well, widow Springy. It looks like you have a king for a mate. But you are now mine. Your favor is to stay with the Rioch nymph coven forever." She smiles. "Swear it."

Kage shifts on his feet and tries to push forward, but it's too late for that. "No, Willow."

I'd love to say the same. *No. Not a chance. Never.* But the magic of the favor is already winding around my tongue. "I swear to stay with the Rioch nymph coven...forever." With a snap of magic, it's done. I now belong to my mate, and a coven of nymphs.

But a hellhound will devour me before I let Ornia have him again.

Chapter Twenty-Five

ONE WAY TRIP

KAGE

If Ornia thinks she can keep me from protecting my mate just because Willow is bound to stay in her coven, she's so very wrong.

I get ready to yell that when the hellhounds step in front of her. Their pinkish-orange eyes home in on me. Drool splatters the ground from the bigger one's gnashing jaws.

"They listen to me, King. But let's be clear. If you do anything too stupid, I'll let them eat you and then your mate will be of no use to me. I won't let them harm her, though. There are so many other things I can use a cutesy little springy for." She shakes Willow.

My heart beats up in my throat. "Stop, Ornia. If she's harmed..." I will not use idle threats. I will show her at my next opportunity.

"What? You'll melt me? Turns out, you've had a sneaky secret magic trick we didn't know about. And now our winter reserves need refilling, which will be the responsibility of the Unseelie."

I huff a laugh. As if she couldn't gather more food than any small fae community would need while she's the size she's in now. And that's not even touching on the broken pact between our kingdoms. "You are absurd."

She narrows her eyes and steps forward, whispering to the fingers not holding Willow.

The hellhounds back away. Was that a coincidence? Actually, there are several things that aren't correct about the hellhounds. To my knowledge, they've only been documented to have black eyes, not orange—the windows looking into the darkest pits of hell, if I remember the description correctly. And they're terrors who will take down prey for the joy of the hunt. They're not... patient. Are these hybrids?

Willow is pale and staring at me. She glances toward Ornia's other hand. Sure enough, there's a sparkle against the nymph's fingertips. I can't see exactly what it is, but I bet it's an enchanted relic.

My mate shifts, pushing at Ornia's fingers. "I can't breathe."

But Willow isn't panicking. I'd feel it as I did during the glamour that slammed into us.

Ornia shrugs, "You'll live. Let's return to the coven."

The nymphs guarding her file away, but keep their weapons trained on me.

"One more thing, if you will, king. Before I let your mate go, I need you to swear not to harm any nymph."

I won't do that—not after everything that happened. But waging a war against all nymphs isn't a move I'll make either. The issue is Ornia, but I can talk her down if I hit the correct accusation.

She's new, powerful with shifting size and enchantments—

I keep my eyes on the hellhounds, who seem to tremble while frozen in front of their mistress. Maybe... "How did you enchant the hellhounds?"

Her eyes narrow the slightest bit before she puffs back up with pride.

I could cheer. My first hit was dead-on. Those who grab power when they don't understand what it means are easy to persuade. They either do the right thing, or to blow themselves up. I don't care which, as long as Willow is safe.

I straighten, lifting my chin as if I'm in my royal robes instead of a sheet-skirt. "And who all knows that you control them?"

Ornia's smug expression drops.

Now I only need to convince this spoiled nymph that her plan is done. I won't bring up that she is also done, though she should expect that.

Willow bares her teeth and jerks her arm from the cage of Ornia's fingers. Her eyes meet mine, pleading with me for something, but I don't know what. But as she inhales, and a snap of magic hits the air, I realize her move.

Ornia jerks and cries out, her head snapping back as she tips, and falls on her ass, sending several nymphs down with her. She screeches and lets go of Willow, who flits through the air to Ornia's other hand.

The hellhounds dash into the woods like they're chasing a pheasant.

I slap away the arrow against me, and the one next to that, and flap to move backwards. "You harm me and there will be no hope for any of you. Ornia has gotten you all into serious trouble. Let us go."

"She'll kill us," the closest nymph whispers.

"I'll kill you," I say, my demon voice coming through.

The nymph in front of me winces, then glances to the one next to her.

Willow darts towards me. "Go!"

I run, knowing my mate will easily catch up since she's flying.

"Stop him," Ornia yells.

Not them, just me. Because my mate can't leave.

Fuck. I slow. "Willow. We have to resolve this."

She slams into me, kissing me and shoving something in my hand. Two somethings. When she moves back, she gives me a sad smile. "Run."

"I'm not able to leave you."

The ground dips.

"You have to," she says. "I love you, Kage." She flits backward before I can hug her to me.

The ground grabs hold of my ankles and pulls.

Just before I go under completely, Ornia slaps Willow from the air.

"No—" My voice is silenced by earth as my brother's magic sucks me underground. There's no stopping the pull, though I kick out, trying to work my way back.

I needed to speak with Ornia when she's not in confrontational mode, but that's over. There's no way Ornia didn't injure Willow with that blow, but I don't feel panic or her leaving my soul. My mate isn't dead.

She better not be dead.

Bursting from the ground, I spit dirt. "No." I thrust my hands into the closing ground, but it pushes me out.

"Kage!" My brother's voice sounds through my panic. He grabs my shoulder and swings me around, dragging me into a hug. A naked hug. My sheet was lost when I was sucked into the ground.

I hug him back hard, then push him away. "I have to go back. Send me back." I signal toward Gentry Vemmi.

He unties his tunic and passes it over.

Typhon furrows his eyebrows and shakes his head. "Why is everyone asking for that? Are you okay, brother?" He looks over me, eyes concerned.

Guards are there too, looking relieved, but also confused.

I shrug into the garment, inhaling the rich flora of my kingdom. My people. I'm home. But it's not where I need to be.

They can wait another day.

"Ornia has declared herself queen of the nymphs and entrapped me using the nymph's kiss. When you sent Willow..." I try to run my hand through my hair, but it gets stuck in dirty tangles.

Typhon nods, his golden hair looking perfect as usual.

A Seelie flying from the direction of the Keep lands behind him. She's shorter than Willow, and curvier, but they both have somewhat similar wings, though this Seelie's have a bluish tint. She smells like flowers but also like mineral water and Typhon.

"Princess Ember," I say, bowing my head.

She curtsies and moves closer. "King Kage. Nice to meet you. Willow?"

"Ornia has her. She made her swear to stay with the coven forever."

Ember tilts her head. "Will she enjoy that?"

"She's my mate."

Everyone's eyes widen.

I nod. "Instantaneous. She broke Ornia's spell over me."

"That nymph really had the audacity to enchant you to stay with her?" Typhon's eyes go red.

I wave him off. "There are so many things I endured she will pay for. But, they injured my mate, and we need to move fast and intelligently. Where's Auralia?"

"The dungeon," Typhon nearly whispers.

Safety never came for us, so neither did Willow's secrets. I could punch a tree right now, but only take a deep breath. "Come with me and explain. I need my second." I rub my chest, feeling like Willow is residing under my breastbone, but that's not close enough. "I need to bathe and review nymph law. We have much to catch up on." I start off toward the keep.

"What are you going to do?" Ember asks, sliding her hand into Typhon's as she flutters to keep up with Typhon and my quick steps.

I look at the two items Willow shoved at me, and abruptly halt. My brilliant mate. "I'm going to turn back into a king, so I may speak with a goddess."

Chapter Twenty-Six

BREATHING SUCKS

WILLOW

"What did you do?" Ornia screeches.

I'd laugh, but I'm too busy trying to suck in enough air to live, and in too much pain to want to do that. The human-sized nymph slapped me out of the air, which hurt. The tree that stopped my trajectory hurt way more. I'm fortunate I mostly hit it with my torso, the strongest part of my body. I don't need a broken leg or wing with no healer around.

Ornia comes toward me, eyes wild and darting around. I use what's left of my magic to punch at her. She screams, then the nymphs around her gasp and back away.

Between the trees, the hellhounds creep forward, low to the ground. They're hunting.

I bare my teeth and launch myself upright, stretching to expand my lungs. Nothing pops or crunches, so that's good. The tree bark scraped my shoulder so badly, spots of dark purple stain my gray tunic over the stinging injury. I'm sore, but not broken. I give my wings a testing flit, and they're okay too, thank the goddess. Half crawling, half flying, I dart upwards.

"Kill her," Ornia screams.

I move faster, waiting for the sting of arrows as I make haste for the cover of branches and leaves.

"But we can't." The whispered voice belongs to Kissip, the nymph who introduced me to Kage. "The King will kill us all if we hurt her. You said that yourself."

"I don't care. He's no match for us."

Another nymph pipes in. "You have minimal magic in that size, and we're no match for the Unseelie army, no matter how good Lillo's glamours are. They will kill us all, Ornia."

I reach a branch and crouch, my back against the trunk.

The pale body of a hellhound prowls through the brush, close to Ornia, but the other is missing. Does she still command them? What if I sent Kage back to his court with nothing of use?

"You will address me as Queen."

Kissip moves backwards, quickly, and keeps her voice low. "Well then, *your majesty*, you should move instead of yapping. Or not." She turns and runs.

And that's when I see the other hellhound.

The beast launches from the tree next to mine, and latches onto Ornia's leg, dragging the screaming nymph toward the thicket near the berry bush that sustained me and Kage. I guess the small locket with the orange gem was the right thing to steal and send with Kage, though now...

I crinkle my nose as the other hellhound scrambles from the forest and goes for Ornia's throat. They're small compared to her, but she doesn't have a chance against thier immense combined strength and mouths full of fangs that are nothing like Kage's.

The other nymphs run, and the tug of my promise compels me to follow. What a mistake I made letting my need for retribution overshadow logic. I didn't prepare for a different future from the one I'd planned. And now I've linked myself to a place I don't want to be.

Pushing myself off the tree, I wince at the snort and snarl and crunch of bone as Ornia's screaming abruptly stops. I take to the air toward my latest fate.

The nymphs are easy to catch up to, as they're wingless, though it's a struggle to stay airborne. I'm tired, injured, and worried about my mate.

Will he even return for me now that he's free of this wretched place? Would I return if my mate acted as I did—holding information from him and not taking his wants into account? I don't know anymore. If I were deceived in the same manner, I'd have a hard time feeling as if the other person cared for me at all.

He shouldn't come back. He should run his keep like the King I've heard he is—diplomatic, but warm. Fair and lawful. Keenly intelligent. I would have liked to have seen him in court, to pretend as if I belonged by his side.

By the time we see the line of huts, we're all breathless. Nymphs hobble and sit on the ground to rest. We stay silent. The area looks even worse than when Kage melted the storage buildings. It looks like the rain the nymph's called for flooded the forest and the coven's town. Mud cakes the huts, as well as furniture stacked in broken piles.

"Did Ornia flood you?" I whisper.

Kissip huffs. "She did." She licks her lips and pushes herself off the ground. "Now, she's gone. If we fight about who's going to rule, the hellhounds will get here quicker to take us out as well. We need food and shelter. Who's doing what?"

"I'm leaving," a nymph with green tendrils of hair says, turning on her heel.

Kissip laughs. "To where? You think the elves will take you in? The other nymph covens?" She waves a hand in my direction. "You think the Seelie and Unseelie haven't heard about what Ornia set up yet? Even the Brownie-kin left our territory when she made the pact. No. We're stuck. We need to live through these next few days and hope the hellhounds get bored and head home."

"What pact?" I ask.

Kissip narrows her eyes. "Do not push me today, Springy. You've done enough."

I shake my head. "By freeing a captured king you enchanted. Did you enjoy yourselves, carving into his wings?"

She winces. "I did not do that."

"You let it happen. That alone is disgraceful."

"He's really your mate?"

I lift my chin. "Yes."

She shakes her head. "I can imagine that was not an easy thing to see."

"It wasn't an easy thing to see when I hated him. But now? I hope each of you gets eaten one by one." I kick off the ground and perch on top of a lopsided hut, hugging my knees to my chest.

"Leave her be." A nymph says when Kissip tries to follow me. "She probably only thinks they're mates. He was with Ornia."

I'd explain more about how the magic of our budding bond tore apart the enchantment, but a growl in the distance spikes fear through my chest.

I'm glad Kage isn't here, but I wish above everything that I was with him. I want his arms around me, and his whispers in my ear. I want his fangs in my neck to prove I am his to his people.

How did my life before Rioch seem like the blink of an eye, and two days act like time expanded just for us? Will I ever see him again?

CHAPTER TWENTY-SEVEN

THE WAIT FOR A GODDESS

KAGE

At the edge of the lake, I peer up at the goddess who glimmers like sun hitting waves. She's staring up at the skies after hearing our story. If we're lucky, she's communicating with others of her kind, but she could be thinking, or letting us wait because time means nothing to deities.

Typhon, Ember, Donovan, and Auralia stand by me. Diplomarians from each Unseelie court stand behind us, except for Ash and Corbin, who have sidled up next to Donovan. Apparently, after assisting our court with the Bogeyman/Auralia incident, they act as though they're part of our court and this situation as well. That keeps me ill at ease, though we may need them if the Lady of the Lake won't help us, and we invade Rioch.

The Enforcer Court keeps their inner workings quiet from the rest of us, and we don't pry because if there's ever a situation like what we've been through lately, they'll send any Unseelie court backup without trying to take over. It's a rare alliance I want to keep.

"Jinimadora should be here," Ash whispers.

I fight rolling my eyes. The fae female that has been our visitor's liaison for a couple of cycles was an assassin from the rogue Unseelie encampments near the dark forest. She's on lockdown in the castle barracks, and I have no idea what to do with her, but it certainly won't be putting her in front of a goddess.

"So she could stab something?" Donovan whispers back.

I snort. *Precisely.*

"Yes." Ash smiles at him, then me. "Maybe it would help move this conversation along."

"Be. Quiet." I glance at the goddess and keep my warm expression on her in case she's somehow paying attention to us as well as the skies.

Ash makes a suffering sigh. "You're not going to execute her, are you?"

"I'm not sure yet." I need more information before I decide.

"You didn't execute your second." Ash raises an arched eyebrow.

"I interpreted the law precisely." I reach to squeeze Auralia's hand. "Though no diplomarian can contest that Auralia's guidance through the cycles hasn't proven her loyalty to the Crown Court."

It wasn't just me who would have fought for her to stay with the court. Besides Donovan—who would have wrecked everyone and everything in his path if we harmed his mate—the entire castle flooded through my chamber to ask me to spare her, though I'd already done so.

Donovan nuzzles at his mate's neck. "It's nice to finally stretch our wings. We're going to go for a long flight after this."

Smiling, I rub at the ache in my sternum. When I get back to Willow, will she allow my mark to solidify an Unseelie mating? If she's okay. That's too painful to think about at the moment. First step, get back to Rioch, and rescue my mate. Then deal with Ornia and throw anyone else who has harmed Willow to the hellhounds. The gem is heavy in the pocket of my formal robes, as I'm sure it is in the pockets of every Unseelie here.

The assembly line to create replicas of the enchanted crystal from dirty stones took far too long, especially as we're not even sure anything but the original will control the beasts. Also, using my magic time after time has tired me. My wish is to curl against Willow in our bed and sleep for days.

But there's no time for that.

"My lady?" I aim at the goddess.

She doesn't flinch.

And we wait some more.

Corbin makes a guttural throat sound and pivots on his heel.

Ash grabs the back of his retreating gentry's tunic and turns him forward again. "Behave or we won't get treats."

"Why must we wait?" Corbin looks about as sour as a troll on a perfect summer day. He is the most undiplomatic gentry of all the courts, but always has Ash with him to speak smoothly.

"Because we must." Ash looks in the same direction as the goddess. "How long do you think it will take to get back to Rioch coven territory?"

My jaw tightens. "A day's flight." For someone who can fly. Typhon will get there long before me, then drag me through the earth. Being separated from the others, then having them breach the territory without me is so wrong, but I haven't been a king for nearly a cycle. What's one more day?

Everything when it comes to getting Willow back.

"Do you have somewhere to be?" Typhon asks Ash. "You've been with us for nearly a moon."

"Nowhere to be, and yet, getting home will be very interesting if we gain what we need."

"Ash," Corbin grumbles.

"Yes, my liege? We've waited for too long, yes? Let me make the deal."

"No."

The goddess shifts, tilting her head.

I clear my throat. "While this is fascinating, we may have an answer." I point to the goddess, who inhales and blinks. "When this is over, I will be glad to hear of your requests."

The goddess we know as the Lady of the Lake looks down at me with moss green eyes.

Water bubbles and swirls beside her before a figure rises, making us all take a collective step back. Before us stands a woman with deep umber skin and nearly black eyes. She's wrapped in what looks like kelp and seagrass.

The Lady of the Lake bows her head. "Welcome, Doris."

My eyes widen as others gasp and drop to their knees.

The ancient creator of the nymphs stands before us.

I step forward and bow. "Goddess."

She moves from the water—or the water lifts her, moving her toward the bank we stand on. As she steps onto the grass, she shrinks until she's my height. Now I know where the nymphs inherited that trait. "Are you the one who claims my daughters are misbehaving?"

Chapter Twenty-Eight

TEAMWORK

WILLOW

I reach down, grasping Kissip's hand and dragging her to a higher branch.

The nymph above us peeks out from behind the trunk, seven branches up. "Hurry." Her voice is as meek as she is, surprising considering the dark glamours she wields.

We move upwards in a silent tandem effort before I drop lower to pull another to safety for a few moments at least.

Three days ago, I might have stood idly by and watched the hellhounds eat them all. By the curse of Hades, the beasts nearly have. But we're exhausted, destitute, and do not know the fate of the others the beasts separated us from in the territory, though it's likely they've fallen and their numbers are as few as ours. These nymphs hurt—the soul type of loss. I've experienced that, and I mourn with them.

But, while I'm without my mate, which is devastating, Kage is alive. He's safe. His soul remains entwined with mine, and while our separation is painful, I'm grateful for his presence. It gives me the slightest hope.

The nymphs I'm with are not so lucky. The beasts hunting us in this forest pick off their sisters, lovers, and best friends each hour, each day, because I was right all along. Hellhounds are looming death. I took away thier chains when I sent the amulet with Kage. Now, the beasts kill for the game of it, and all we can do is try to survive as they clear our numbers from this forest.

The coven sisters share whatever food we can gather as we run. They watch out for me as if I were one of them and didn't send the only way to control the beasts with my mate down a hole in the ground. While I believe the nymph's acceptance is strategic because I can fly and scout for them, after yesterday morning, they've given me a new appreciation for how a real family operates.

I've learned much about their kind. Not all of them can change sizes easily or at all. Most need to be around those whose stature they wish to mimic, as if their magic needs to explore the size in person before igniting. The goddess blessed Ornia with the ability to alter herself without an example.

Unfortunately for them all, her ambition grew too great. She forgot the others needed her skills, not her manipulations. She acted alone, her excitement to rule overshadowing friends and family, laws and goodwill. With the trouble she has caused, she has shamed all nymphs.

Kissip told me they didn't know what else to do but see how things played out. They're meant for pleasure, not war. And Ornia thrust them into a situation they had no experience in. They were not pre-pared, and she made it seem like such an intelligent, simplistic move. She made it seem fun.

And they've paid so heavily.

I nearly have as well.

Yesterday at sunset, I was pinned, jammed between rocks that one hellhound was moving aside to get to me. Just as the barrier shifted, a nymph threw herself in the path between me and death, telling me in her last second before jaws clamped over her body that I was important. I could save the others better than anyone.

My family would have run in the other direction, glad for the distraction my body provided.

My former mate would have been happy to be free of me.

Yet a nymph met her end for me and her remaining coven-mates. I can't curse at the nymphs when they sacrifice themselves without hesitation for each other and for me. And with that, damn her, she gave me purpose.

I am a protector—always have been. And I am important.

So, I drag another exhausted nymph up higher, my muscles straining, my back sore and weak. We need food and shelter, but we're alive. For now.

A growl in the forest makes us freeze. Then a snort to our right has us looking toward the hellhound that is too close and eyeing us.

The nymph tries to let go of my hand. "Fly," she whispers.

I stare into her icy blue eyes and smile. "It's too late."

The beast is right there. I only wish Kage wouldn't feel the loss of our bond. It hurts to be alone. It might hurt more if a remnant of me remains in his soul—a reminder of our short time together.

"Lillo." Kissip sobs her coven sister's name from five branches up. She knows. We're done.

The beast stalks forward within snapping distance but freezes when another growl sounds from the depths of the woods. Or was it more of a whine? That's probably just my panic messing with my senses. The hellhound turns its head, and I jerk at the nymph's hand, dragging her up, while fluttering my wings as fast as possible. We make it up two branches before the hellhound whips its head back toward us and bares its teeth.

Bright orange spills into its black eyes, but then it takes off into the woods. I had to have imagined it. Maybe it's crunching my bones now, and this is my brain coping with the pain in the last moments of life.

Kissip drops from the branches to hug us, shocking me into reality. She pulls at us. "Higher. It will come back. The other…" She sniffles. "The other probably caught someone."

I squeeze her shoulder. "Higher is good." We can get a few moments of sleep on a wide branch, a nest, or tree notch. We're starving, and if I rest, I can find a berry or at least an edible flower for us to share in the seconds it will take a hellhound to find me.

"Willow?" Kage's voice calls out.

I huff as I leap to the air to join Kissip on the branch above me. "I need food. I'm hallucinating."

"Willow." She points toward the forest floor.

I follow her signal and see a mirage.

It's Kage, but he's in a cloak of purple and he has a shining bronze crown haloing his hair that flows over his shoulders in golden waves. He's so beautiful.

"Kage?" I ask.

"Come here," he says with desperation, reaching upwards towards me.

I turn to Kissip. "You see him?"

"Yes. Go." She pushes at me before dropping to the branch below us. "The hellhounds?"

"Are contained." Kage steps closer to the tree. "Don't make me come up there, mate. My wings are still healing."

I gasp and leap from the tree. I'm barely able to slow before I crash into his arms.

"Willow," he whispers as he holds me with crushing force.

"Nymphs," a demanding feminine voice calls behind us.

Kissip and the others slowly approach, heads bowed.

Lillo drops from two branches up and yelps when she hits the forest floor.

I push from Kage's arms and flutter to her, helping her up. "Broken?"

She shakes her head but stays low and crawls toward the woman.

I flutter to stand between the nymphs and the female. "What do you want?" I point at her. "If you're going to come in here and act like Ornia did with them, you're wrong."

The woman raises her eyebrows.

"Willow, stop." Kage steps beside me, tugging me against him.

I'm too weak to resist. "They won't follow another like they did her. They need rest and to regroup."

The woman's parted lips tip up. "I see what you mean, King." She moves forward like she's floating. "Greetings, Seelie Willow. I am Doris."

I don't know who Doris is, and look to Kissip for answers, but she's crouched, forehead on the ground.

Kage tugs my chin so I'll face him. "The goddess mother of all nymphs."

I scrunch my nose. So much for being a king's diplomatic bride. Is that what I am? He's here, but was it to seek revenge or see me? I lean against him, inhaling his scent in case it's the last time, but it's now mixed with something spicy and decadent that makes my mouth water.

"Ornia is dead," I say. "The hellhounds took her first."

"Shame," the goddess Doris says. "I would have enjoyed punishing her myself. You four, we have much to discuss. With me."

Kissip's face is a mask of pain as she hobbles to her bloody feet.

"They're starving," I blurt, wincing again. "Apologies for my brashness, but we've been running for days with little food, no supplies, and only fear on our minds. There were many lost, and that takes a toll as well."

"Yes." Doris pulls five green, circular items from the odd wet robes she wears, handing one to each of us.

I watch Kissip bow again and bite into the disk, then follow suit. It's salty, but edible, and I'm far too hungry to be concerned with the taste.

"Now we speak." The goddess pivots and floats through the forest with the others on her heels.

I'm compelled to follow, a frustration that makes me grumble.

Kage clears his throat. "Goddess. If you will."

She pauses and turns. "Oh, yes. Seelie Willow, you're released from your oath with the blessings of the nymphs. King, leave the locket unless you'd like to be consumed by brimstone in the next short moments."

Pulling out the locket I shoved into his hands, Kage takes a last look at it, then tosses it to the ground. "I'm sure the hounds' caretakers will be glad to have them returned."

Doris hums. "As will my daughters. Go, King. And if we meet again, may it be on better terms."

Kissip nods at me.

"Still planning to visit?" I call out.

"Expect me at some point, Springy." She waves and continues following her goddess.

I turn into Kage's chest, clutching the soft material of his shirt. I must look like a wretch, but he cups my cheek and sets his forehead to mine. "You scared me, mate."

Too choked up for words, I nod.

"Next time you decide to be noble, you better not throw me down a tunnel."

I rub my nose against his. "Then don't put yourself into situations where I need to throw you down a tunnel."

He grins and kisses my forehead. "In the darkest times, you're still stubborn."

"But still alive." My words are thick.

"I knew you were. My intelligent, strong mate. Let's go home."

"Home?"

Kage takes my hand, walking me toward a crowd of Unseelie scattered between trees. They all bow at us—at me—as we pass.

CHAPTER TWENTY-NINE

BATHED IN EXHAUSTION

KAGE

Willow fell asleep in my arms long before I stepped into our room. She remained that way as I drew a bath and settled us in to soak, though she briefly woke, told me to not fall off the tree and passed back out against my chest.

The water is growing cold as Ember peeks around the door frame. "She okay?"

I tuck Willow's wet curls behind her ear. "Are you going to wake up for us, Queen? The water's getting chilled."

Willow sighs and rubs her cheek against my chest, then turns her face and goes back to sleep.

I shrug. "She's so exhausted. I hate it took so long to get to her. She could have…" I scrunch my nose. She'd been running from hellhounds for days. They could have gotten to her before I did. I could have walked back into Rioch and found nothing.

"But she didn't." Ember steps in. "May I?" She points to the bottles of oils and soaps.

"Go ahead. I doubt she'll wake."

The princess flutters over, taking a bottle of soap oil and drizzling it over Willow's curls. "I didn't know she harbored such resentment. I wouldn't have sent her."

"I'm glad you did. I'd still be there, and my mate wouldn't be using me as a pillow." I smile and cup my hand, dousing her hair with bath water. "Any news from your mother?"

Ember massages Willow's curls. "She told me she relayed to Willow what she heard about Flint, and when I pressed to know why she kept the information from me, she told me to leave it be and she wouldn't be speaking of it further." The princess pitches her voice up. "'It's the past, daughter. Leave it be.'"

"I'm not surprised." It's clear the Spring Seelie Queen either didn't have the means or the want to look into what happened and rehashing will put her in a precarious position, making her people distrustful of her—which they should be. "What do you think happened to Willow's mate?"

Ember's lips twist to the side as she works on my mate's hair. "He's out there. And the more I ponder about it, the more I believe Bogen was involved. I'll ask a few new friends who were also trapped under the boggart's deception. Some were there a long while. They may remember Flint."

"Do you remember him?"

She raises her eyebrows, but nods. "He was very...confident. Not so much attractive as personable. And he was attentive to Willow when they came to events and such. I wouldn't have known there was anything untoward between them, though once they bonded, he wasn't around as much."

"She enjoys attending events?" I stroke my thumb over Willow's cheek.

"She was at every one. She'd come out on her own, dressed up..." Ember flicks her eyebrows as she oils and combs through Willow's tangles. "Captivating. She was dazzling long before Flint. Thinking back on it, she started to dull before he disappeared."

That doesn't surprise me. I'll throw my mate a ball when she's ready. Several of the royal clothiers will speak with her about what she'd like to wear for events and around the castle. No more gray frocks.

Ember finishes combing through Willow's hair and stands. "Think you can manage from here?"

"I'm not sure anyone can manage this Seelie."

She laughs. "You're not incorrect."

I tip Willow back as Ember helps rinse my mate's hair. "Thank you for being here. Now and while I was gone."

Ember flutters to the door. "I like this kingdom and your Unseelie. They're fun."

"They are. It will be nice getting to know you, Princess."

She curtsies. "And you, King."

"Tell my brother to put Donovan and Auralia on setting a date and staff for a ball."

"Will do."

And I'm alone again with my exhausted mate. "What am I going to do with you, my flower?"

Chapter Thirty

THE NEW ROOM

KAGE

A gasp brings me upright.

"What is it?" I ask, squinting at the bright light in the room from the open curtains.

"Mushroom?" Willow says—or I think she says, but her mouth is full.

I chuckle and drop back onto my fluffy pillow. "I assume you approve."

"Delicious. What is this?" She holds up a cylindrical vegetable.

"Seared radish. How are you feeling?"

Holding a blanket around her, she nibbles the vegetable, then puts it down and snatches another mushroom chunk. "Better. Mother of Hades, is this hibiscus tea?" She inhales against the cup.

I grin at her pleasured hum. "You can thank Ty for that. They don't grow in our area."

She squeaks when she tastes it.

"Fuck. You're so sweet, Willow." I beckon her with a finger. "Hurry up and eat, so I can eat you." Acknowledging that I missed her is an understatement. I've yearned for her with my entire soul.

Her eyebrows rise as she licks her fingers. Color is back in her skin and her hair is shiny and riotous around her. She looks rested and happy, though not happy enough.

My cock springs to life, and I roll, crawling across the bed to swipe at my mate.

She dodges and takes a sip. "I'm drinking tea."

"Put down the tea." My voice rumbles and I lick my fangs.

Her wings buzz and her lips part, eyes ablaze with a deep purple hue, but she takes another step back. "Or what?"

I flap my wings and leap.

She squeaks again and drops the cup.

I catch it midair, licking the spilled drop from the side before taking a sip, then offer it back to her, but swipe her blanket as she takes it from me. I loop my arm around her bare waist and nuzzle her neck. "Enjoy your tea, my queen, while I enjoy you."

She stretches to put the cup on the side table. "Kage?"

Her neck is soft, and she smells like honey mixed with her fresh floral scent. I hum in question.

"This isn't a dream, right? You came to get me out of the Rioch forest and I'm at the Crown Court Keep?"

"Yes." I tighten my hold on her, trailing my tongue up to her ear. "You're here with me."

"Am I yours?"

I lean back to look at her, gripping her chin with two fingers. "Yes. And I am yours. Are you ready for me to court you?"

She bites her lip. "You ask me while naked with your cock in my hand."

"My cock is not—" I gasp as she wraps her fingers around me and squeezes. I bare my fangs at her as she gives me slow, teasing strokes. "I asked if you're ready for me to court you?"

"Can we skip all that and I'll just be yours?"

I shake my head. "May I court you, Willow?"

She purses her lips in thought, maybe considering what it's going to be like as a queen or if our Unseelie will accept her. It's hard to tell what goes on in that clever mind. "Are you sure?"

I take her face in both my hands and nod. "Yes. What's the hesitation?"

"If you change your mind?"

"I won't."

She rolls her eyes. "I don't want you locked in something you find you don't want."

"Willow. Do you want to be with me? Here?" I look to our room of decadent silken fabrics and cranberry-stained teakwood. "Is the room a problem? The castle? The Unseelie?" I can't change who I am for her, but I certainly need to know if it is an issue between us.

She shakes her head. "I'm just afraid. If there's any part of you that doesn't want me..."

I lift her and turn toward the bed. "There's not. If you wish to expand our courtship to make sure of both our intentions, I will. Time will help prove I am yours." I settle her on the bed and press against her, pinning her so that I can kiss her sweet lips a thousand times.

"Kage," she whispers when I move my lips along her jaw.

My fangs extend when I trace my tongue along her neck, but I ignore the call. She's not ready; she may never be, but we're bonded, even if it's not exact or if she has doubts.

"Okay," she whispers, tilting her chin up. "I trust you."

My lips freeze on her neck, then I pull back to stare at her, gorgeously spread out under me. "What?"

"Okay. I can't deny you. I don't want to."

I thumb her cheeks. "Did I woo you?"

She tilts her head. "Woo?"

Using my most charming purr, I brush my lips over hers. "Yes. Are you sufficiently wooed, my flower?"

"Oh." Her eyes light up. "We're doing this now?"

I nod. "As soon as you're ready, I want to make it official." I tap her nose. "Are you wooed?"

"I remember this from the Springfest Sprint." Her lips firm and her brows angle in a serious expression. She nods. "Yes, Kage, you have wooed me."

"Good." I back away from her and cross the room to pull the chunk of tanzanite I brought up from the gem room because it reminded me of Willow. I glide back over, pinning her under me again, and hold up the gem. "Please accept this gift as a token of my intentions and love for you. If you accept it, I'll have it set in your crown."

Her lips part as she eyes the stone. Then she blinks her glassy eyes at me and swallows. "Love?"

Nuzzling her cheek, I nod. "You think you're the only one who can say it? I heard you as Ty's magic sucked me into the ground. Yes, my flower. I love your passion, cleverness, and even that stubborn streak because it exists out of concern for others. You are exceptional, my mate. How could I not love you?" I swipe an escaped tear from her cheek and sniffle away my own.

"I never thought I could feel as loved as I do when I'm with you. I accept."

"Then kiss me."

She grabs my face and presses her lips to mine for a hard, needy kiss. When she drops back again, she maneuvers a leg from under me and wraps it over my hip. "I, Willow Shadeleaf Frindotild, am yours, King Kage Brightline Jenderos."

I smile. "You remembered." She'd said she knew of our customs, but I only shared my name once.

"I did." She bites her lip.

"Well, Willow Shadeleaf Frindotild, there's only one thing left to do."

She blows out a breath and tilts her chin up. "Do it."

Not when she's trembling and fearful of what my fangs can do. I kiss her neck, cup her backside, and slide my cock slowly into her.

She clutches at me and whimpers.

Balancing on my elbow, I bring her hand to my lips. "Feel." I lick her finger, then suck it. Her pussy clenches around me, and I smile, showing off my fangs that are aching for her.

Her breaths coming in short bursts as her hips shift beneath me. She touches my left fang. Her lips part, and she taps the middle of her upper lip with her tongue. It turns her on. As if her buzzing wings give her away, and she slickens further for me.

I lick a fang and her finger. "You fucking love them. Beg me."

She raises her eyebrows. "Bite me."

I growl. "You can do better than that."

There's no hesitation as she whispers, "Please?"

I hum. "I need you to tell me exactly what you want from me."

"I want you to take my neck."

"Now put that all together. How much do you want my fangs, Willow? I need to know you want me—us."

She licks her lips and presents her neck to me. "Please take my neck, my king. I want you. I want your mark." She has no idea what her words, her need, does to me.

I slow my thrusts and kiss where I'm going to mark my mate. Her skin is warm and her scent blooms. Gripping a handful of her curls, I press my fangs to her and wait, giving her one last moment to deny or prepare.

"Kage, I swear if you don't—"

I sink in, both my fangs and my cock, slow and deep.

Willow keens and digs her nails into my back as her hips grind into mine. There's no holding back my orgasm as she rhythmically pulses around my cock and her blood and magic hits my tongue, snapping through me and tightening our already-solid bond.

"Kage," she whimpers.

I grumble against her neck, then slowly retract, lick, and kiss the slight wound. "Willow," I say with a smile, "was it as terrible as you thought it would be?"

"Every terrible thing about you turns out to be my favorite thing." She reaches toward her neck.

"Not yet." I snatch her hand. I don't want her to see more blood or injury, even if it feels good.

In true Willow fashion, she ignores me, and swipes at the punctures, pulling her fingers up to look. In complete disregard for my lust, she licks them.

I grip under her knee and thrust back in, already hard. "We're not leaving this room for a full moon."

She pushes my shoulder, so I tuck my wings and turn to my back, taking her with me. She rolls her hips, showing off her stunning beauty and confidence. "And then we're having a ceremony of binding, so that my family and all Spring Seelie see that I'm yours and no one else's."

I purr at the thought of such a public display of our togetherness. "Anything you want is yours, Queen. Especially that."

CHAPTER THIRTY-ONE

EPILOGUE

WILLOW

Kage and I walk hand-in-hand between the crowds of Seelie, Unseelie, and a variety of fae folk that were invited to Nameless Pass to witness our formal binding. When he said he wanted the entire realm to witness our union, I didn't know he meant the literal entire realm.

Though this move was also strategic.

Typhon bonding with Ember was one thing, but the King of the illustrious Crown Court taking a Seelie Queen? One that's not even royal? There are more than a few sour faces, especially the Queen of the West Wind Court, the smallest of the Unseelie courts. She's always thought Kage would eventually give in to her pestering and bind with her, uniting to offset the balance in the Unseelie realm.

The royals of the Enforcer Court are not present. Kage didn't seem surprised that they decided not to show, though we left additional guards at the keep, just in case. Kage relaxed when Ash waved from behind Donovan. The Grimm brothers seem to be set on keeping their alliance with our court.

Kage squeezes my hand when I glance his way. Our bond thrums hot within my soul, making me even more sure that this unexpected path is what I'm meant to travel. "You look stunning, my queen."

"I feel stunning." My dress is layers of bright teal and celadon silk with velvety violet petals.

Auralia and Donovan put my hair half up in intricate braids that highlight the crown Kage had made for me.

Ember dusted my skin with sparking moth scales.

And though I look like a queen, it's Kage's actions that make me feel worthy of him. Our full moon shut in turned into two moons. We weren't ready to face the responsibilities that would take away from our time together.

During that time, he told me everything about his kingdom—the good, the bad, and the terribly painful. He's shown me more trust than any being I've ever met. And he's sought my opinions about it all, as if this was a role I was built for. Maybe I was, because while my start with Kage and the Unseelie began in deception, now that I have all the information and have let go of the past—now that I'm treated not as a wound but as a stitch—I will fight with everything I am to keep my mate and kingdom safe.

The only family I have present is a cousin from the summer court. She told me my parents and siblings believed the letter sent from the Unseelie kingdom was a trap, though I'm unsure what they possess that would require a trap to lure them out. Hatred, favor debt, and spite? That's all they're blessed with. Though maybe they thought my past mate was luring them out to get even with the favor our families tied us together with.

When Kage and I sought information about Flint, we concluded we may never know what happened to him or where he is now, if he's alive. I find I don't mind it. There are other, more pressing matters than a past that hurt me more than helped me.

Reaching up, I cup my mate's cheek. "When do we get to go home?"

The gloriously boyish way he has when he looks at me has my stomach fluttering. "Are you impatient, mate?" Dipping, he whispers in my ear. "What's your pleasure this evening? Wax? A switch perhaps?"

The memory of his rippling, sweat-slick muscles as he reddened nearly all of my skin before making the sweetest love to me makes my channel clench in want.

I grip his velvety shirt and go on tiptoes to whisper back. "Perhaps the switch and some rope...on *you* this evening."

He growls low in his throat.

"Before you two meander off"—Ash stares at us with a raised eyebrow—"let's speak of our payment."

"Ash," Kage groans. "Must we do this now?"

"Well, since you two rarely make it five steps from your bedroom, you've been a little difficult to pin down for a discussion. I'll make this quick. We will be accepting your captive, Jinimadora, and her family as payment for our recent services." He holds up a finger as Kage inhales to speak. "I understand this is not a typical request—"

"Or a lawful one," Auralia says, stepping next to Kage.

Ash smiles. "Which we will be happy to discuss in, oh, let's say, three moons from now, when the binding of Corbin and Jinimadora is complete."

I raise my eyebrows and glance at Kage, who appears just as shocked.

Ash nods. "Wild, right? At that time, we will be so happy to have your presence at the Enforcer Keep." There's something about his expression that is almost vulnerable or asking. Like he wants involvement but can't say the words. "Corbin and I will take care of her, and, as another quick request, her family will stay with your court until the binding ceremony. Can we trust you with that?"

My mate appears calm and happy, though my soul tells me he's on guard. "You ask if you can trust *us* when you're requesting that we give you an Unseelie to pay a favor?"

"Not requesting." Ash is back to his typically jovial self. Then he steps closer, and black bleeds into his blue eyes, sending a chill into my stomach. I've never seen an Unseelie's eyes do that. His voice lowers. "Let's be clear. We need her. Your trust in me—in what Corbin and I have done for you—will be repaid."

I know fear when I see it, black eyes or not. "Do you need help, Ash? What's—"

He puts a finger over his lips and blinks. His eyes shift back into vibrant blue as he lowers his hand. "None of us should stand in the way of love, yes? Feast. Celebrate. We'll see you all soon enough."

"And how long until you collect this favor?" Kage asks.

Typhon steps close behind him, putting a hand on his brother's shoulder.

Taking a step back, Ash bows. "Tis' already done. Congratulations to you both. Truly."

He pivots and disappears into the crowd, leaving the rest of us looking at each other for answers, to which we have none.

"Check the Keep," Kage whispers.

Typhon squeezes his shoulder and heads toward the tree line with Ember, the gentry, and a guard.

Kage palms my hip and whispers, "There may be more than the An Nasc Iontach to worry about."

"Appears so." I kiss the purple robes covering his shoulder. "Should we go?"

"No. It's our wedding day. A time of peaceful celebration." He lifts me and spins me around, though the slightest furrow remains on his forehead. This is what being royalty is like—holding all the information and pretending you don't.

I giggle and wrap my arms around his neck. "Do you think the great heat will affect us?"

Kage nods. "I think it will affect all fae, and only the gods know how."

"When you spoke to Doris, did you mention it?"

He huffs a short laugh. "I did. And she ignored me."

I shake my head. "Goddesses."

"Indeed."

He strokes my cheek, turning my face to his, then presses a sweet kiss to my lips. "There will be troubles sometimes, but nothing we can't handle together."

I glance around the crowd and process the surreal notion that he's right. I am right where I should be. Together with Kage. Part of something great.

I nuzzle his cheek. "Let's be together with this group, then together alone, then together while protecting what's ours."

He hugs me and whispers in my ear. "We'll do it all, my flower."

NEXT UP...

The next book in the series is A Grim Proposal.
Sign up for Poppy's newsletter and receive a free Faetales Itty Bitty story, Go Ahead And Steal My Heart.

Copyright © 2025 by Poppy Minnix – Follow the QR code

About the Author

Poppy Minnix

Poppy Minnix is an award-winning author of mythology romantasy and contemporary romance. She loves to reimagine the world with ancient myths present, then dash in some spice and humor. Her characters are hot messes who find their perfect fit in life and in romance. You will find an escape, hidden strength, intriguing and diverse characters, and overcoming shame or guilt in her books.

She lives in Maryland with a husband who is far more romantic than she is, kids, pets, and plants—everything she immensely loves.

Find more about her on socials and her newsletter.

Poppy Minnix
www.poppyminnix.com
poppymwrites@gmail.com

Acknowledgements

Mary! I can't appreciate you more with all the amazing things you do for me and others. You are such a rockstar!

Thanks to my Inkerscon/mastermind gang for having all the answers, assistance, and accountability a gal could want. I'm lucky to have found you!

Thanks to the ARC readers who let me know about pesky typos that love to sneak by all edits. Everyone appreciates you!

Dearest reader! Thank you for the notes, reviews, and social media conversations. While being an author is just the best, it can also be really hard. Thanks for reminding me why I write. And thanks for sharing my love of spicy fae romantasy. I'm glad we have each other!